BLACK COBRA

~~~~~~~~~

JOHN AVERY

San Diego, California

4th Edition, April 2013

Published by Apticon Books
United States of America
ISBN: 978-0-9836963-3-9

For
Arthur and Kathryn
To whom I owe so much

"Every man's life ends the same way. It is only the details of how he lived and how he died that distinguish one man from another."

– Earnest Hemingway

PREFACE

During the Cold War Seventies and Eighties, Soviet submarines regularly patrolled the Pacific Coast of North America. By international treaty, intrusions into the USA's territorial waters were strictly forbidden; however, the "Project 641" *Foxtrot*-class diesel-electric attack sub, one of the largest non-nuclear submarines ever built, was one of the quietest submarines in the Soviet fleet, and rumors of numerous incursions persist to this day.

Now, less than 30 years after the collapse of the Berlin Wall signaled the end of the Cold War, there are only a handful of Soviet-era attack submarines in existence, and most are permanently moored, as tourist attractions, along the world's big-city waterfronts, including several in America.

One of these infamous "Project 641" attack submarines — b-39, code name Cobra — undoubtedly stalked many of the U.S. Navy's ships home ported in San Diego, and is now berthed, amidst her former adversaries, on San Diego Bay (a popular international cruise ship destination and home of close to one third of the United States Naval Pacific Fleet), as part of the Maritime Museum of San Diego.

That much is fact. What follows is fiction. However, one must wonder if something like this could happen ...

~ THE AFTERMATH ~

FRIDAY
SOMEWHERE ON THE EAST COAST

Chapter 1

Aaron Quinn wiped the condensation from his passenger side window with the sleeve of his heavy wool overcoat and peered into the gloom. Thick clouds once again covered the moon and a light rain dampened the gray urban landscape moving past him, reminding him of a scene from a classic dystopian novel.

He and the three in the Aston Martin with him were in a collective state of shock. The positive glow of adrenaline had worn off, and the enormity of what had happened to them had sunk in.

They had just killed a man. And although the psycho deserved to die, he was dead nonetheless, probably still warm, sprawled on the cold floor back at the rundown, downtown eatery known as Sally's Diner.

Between the passing buildings Aaron could see the southern horizon, still glowing a faint red, as his and his best friend Willy's former hideout, the Alton Brothers Fish Cannery, continued to smolder after the two of them had blown it to bits and burned it to the ground.

Aaron shuddered as once again the memories of the last three days chilled him like ice water through his veins.

Not thirty minutes ago, he and Willy had raced their bikes through the darkening city trying desperately to get to Sally's Diner before it was too late. He could see them throw their bikes to the sidewalk and run to peer through the diner's large front window, hoping to see his mother alive.

He recalled the fleeting joy of seeing her inside, with Michael St. John, then the bloodied face and enraged eyes of their assailant. He could feel the tightness in his throat as he squeezed the trigger, the powerful recoil pushing him back as his and Willy's assault rifles shattered first the diner's plate-glass window then behind it the evil who would have killed them all.

Like rising flood waters, the memories consumed the space around him and he felt that soon he would drown in them like a rat in a rain barrel.

Stop thinking about it, you fool, he told himself. *For God's sake, just look out the window and watch the city go by.*

He blinked hard, trying to squeeze the horrible visions out of his mind, but it was impossible. The memories were too fresh.

Chapter 2

The twenty-five-year-old redhead knockout stood alone in the bathroom of the small apartment, concentrating on the job at hand. She jumped when the door banged open then turned to see the man she had just slept with standing behind her, stark naked.

"Damn you, Jason Beckham," she said. "You want me to break the needle off in my arm?"

"Haven't you had enough, Brandy?" Jason said, disgusted. He stepped around her and checked his medicine cabinet. "I'm fresh out of Naloxone, so you're on your own if you O.D." He turned and walked back into his bedroom.

"I'm doing one lousy deuce, okay?" Brandy said after him. "I'm not an *idiot* — and that was just that one time!" She released the surgical-rubber strap from her arm and tossed it, and the rest of the paraphernalia, into a ziplock bag.

Brandy hated when Jason used his patronizing tone, but at 26, a lean six-foot-two, and stunningly handsome, Jason was a vision Brandy couldn't stay mad at for long.

She followed him into the bedroom, pressing a folded tissue to the inside of her arm. "There's something I'd like to talk to you about," she said.

Jason reached for his jeans. "What, Johnny called and he knows you're screwing around on him?"

"No — *God* no," she said. "Don't even joke about that! You know as well as I do he'd kill us both."

Jason had to admit that was true.

"I had lunch with him today," Brandy said, "and he got drunk and told me he's meeting a woman at Sally's Diner tonight."

"So what?" Jason said.

"Are you even *listening?*" Brandy said. "I can't have Johnny hanging out with *other women.*"

Jason found that amusing, considering what he and Brandy had just done.

"And why would he tell *me* about it?" she went on. "Don't you think that's a little weird?"

She had a point: Brandy and Johnny had been together for years, and as far as Jason knew (and in spite of ample opportunity), Johnny had never strayed. And even if he did he would have spared her feelings and never told her about it in the first place.

"I guess it is a little odd," Jason said. "Who's the woman?"

"I don't know, her name's Ashley Quinn — it doesn't matter. But I have this bad feeling about that meeting, okay? I can't shake the feeling he's in serious trouble."

Jason looked her in the eye and a sudden, visceral unease swept over him. It was common for her to come up with wildly random shit to stress about, and most of it was simply annoying; but for some reason this time he believed her.

"You're serious, aren't you," he said.

"Yes, Jason. I'm serious."

He checked his watch. 6:58 p.m. "What time were they meeting?"

"At 6:30, I think. I already called Needles, and I'm sure he was headed over there. But that was an hour ago. He would have called me back by now — if everything was okay, I mean."

Jason stepped into a pair of sandals, grabbed his sweatshirt-jacket, and without a word walked out of his apartment leaving the door wide open.

Brandy listened as he descended the stairs and exited the decaying building through the front door, and then she went to the window and watched through the rain as he crossed the street and climbed into his black Hummer. Then he drove off toward downtown.

Chapter 3

Aaron Quinn listened as the Aston Martin's wiper blades tapped out their relentless rhythm, hoping to distract himself from the horrifying memories threatening his sanity. He reached for his wallet and pulled out a small photo, the one-of-a-kind shot of his mother hugging his real father, taken when he was nine during a family vacation while his dad was home on furlough the summer before he was killed in action overseas. The priceless photo represented the last days they spent together as a family, and minutes earlier, Aaron had rescued it from the pocket of a bloody corpse.

An only child, Aaron recalled how after his dad died he had attempted to hold his breath long enough to kill himself, concluding that self-suffocation was physically impossible. He often wondered how many other pathetic souls had tried it before resorting to more traditional and reliable suicide techniques. Now, four long years since his father's death, vivid images of those techniques haunted him still.

Aaron was very angry: angry at himself, angry at the world, angry at God for taking his father, and for letting the last three days happen — the last three *horrible* days. He remembered what his father had said to him many years ago: "God doesn't stop bad things from happening, Aaron. He gives us comfort and hope, and the strength to deal with adversity and look for the good."

He glanced at the others. *After all the horrors we've lived through together, I may have the makings for a brand new family here*, he told himself. He smiled at the possibility and put on a happy face for their benefit.

"So, where we headed?" he asked brightly, his question directed at the driver of the car, Michael St. John, whom Aaron had known for just three days, yet loved like a father. It was a good question, and Aaron's beautiful, loving mother, Ashley, and his best friend, Willy, sat up in the back seat and listened for Michael's reply.

Michael checked his watch. 7:05 p.m. He considered Aaron's question for a moment. His immediate goal after leaving Sally's Diner had been to put as much distance between themselves, the dead man, and the approaching sirens as he could. He looked at Aaron, then back at the road, and decided to try a more comforting answer.

"We're headed to a faraway place where no one can bother us ever again," he replied, and Aaron and the others thought that sounded really good.

Ashley had seen Aaron take out the photo of her and Danny. "May I see the picture, Aaron?" she asked over his shoulder, and he handed it to her.

Tears welled in her eyes as she took a long look at the photo, imagining herself wrapped in Danny's loving arms once again.

Just then a large black Hummer moving at high speed skidded wide around the flooded corner ahead of them and crossed into their lane. Aaron caught a fleeting glimpse of the oncoming driver's face just before they collided head-on, sending the Aston spinning violently in a shower of glass. The Hummer zagged hard, jumped the curb, and careened through a street-light pole before crashing to a stop against an overflowing dumpster. The Aston Martin slid to a stop in the middle of the block, doors flung wide open, its fabric top mostly torn away, and for a moment nothing moved except for the falling rain ...

Then *BOOM!*

The Aston's fuel tank blew with enough force to heave the car several feet into the air where it rolled onto its side before returning to earth with a violent *whump,* flames roiling from its shattered windows.

Jason stumbled out of his Hummer, stunned, but unhurt. He approached the Aston's fiery wreckage; but the heat was too extreme and there was nothing he could do, so he backed off.

As he turned back toward his Hummer, Jason was surprised to see what appeared to be a boy, about thirteen, lying in the shadows on the wet sidewalk a few feet from him. The boy's face was blackened and bloody, but he was still breathing and appeared to be in one piece. Jason checked the boy's pulse, finding it weak but steady. He spotted a curious bandage wrapping the boy's chest and shoulder — it was soaked with fresh blood but appeared to be controlling any excessive bleeding.

Jason lifted the boy into his arms and carried him to the Hummer, laying him gently across the wide rear seat and covering him with a wool blanket. Then he swung the door shut.

He checked the front of the Hummer for damage: It was smashed in, but not severely. He climbed into the driver's seat and tried the engine, which started easily, and then he backed away from the dumpster and onto the street, heading west with the intention of finding the nearest hospital.

After rounding two corners, Jason remembered why he'd come downtown in the first place. He pulled over and skidded to a stop in front of Sally's Diner.

In the distance, *sirens* ...

Chapter 4

The old, black, desk phone rang, shaking Detective James Harness out of a good sleep. He checked his watch, 7:10 p.m., and then slid his feet off his desk and sat up, fumbling for the receiver.

"Detective Harness," he said in a gruff voice, pinching the bridge of his nose to help ease his headache.

"Harness, it's your Captain. Several calls just came in concerning gunfire downtown at Sally's Diner, and I guess there's been a fatal automobile accident two blocks from there. You and your partner get your asses down there. Got it? Backup's on the way and emergency services have been notified."

"Roger that, Captain," Harness said, yawning deeply. He'd been cooped up in his hot, tiny office all afternoon and welcomed the evening's first real diversion.

He hung up the phone and called to his partner. *"Roberts? You out there?"*

Officer Roberts was just outside Harness's door in the deserted precinct office refilling his coffee cup. He was nursing a huge hangover and a steady stream of black coffee was the only thing keeping him alive.

"Right here, sir," he replied. "No need to yell."

"Pour me some joe to go and grab your shotgun," Harness ordered. "We have a situation."

Chapter 5

Jason listened to the approaching sirens, judging their distance at two minutes. He pulled his .45 caliber pistol out of the Hummer's glove box and stepped out into the rain.

Brandy Fine had been right to be concerned, the front of Sally's Diner looked like a war zone: the green canvas awning hung in tatters; the huge, plate-glass front window was blown out; and two rusting bicycles lay tangled on the sidewalk amid piles of broken glass.

Jason raised his pistol and stepped cautiously through the shattered window into the diner.

Inside, Jason saw the familiar signs of recent mayhem and brutal violence: fresh blood spattered the floor, walls and ceiling, and the entire room was riddled with bullet holes.

Two bodies lay sprawled on the floor: The first, lying under one of the stools at the counter, appeared to be an old man. Jason tried to check the gentleman's pulse, but the old geezer jerked awake and abruptly stood and wandered out the front door, as if he'd simply finished his donut and was heading home.

Jason turned to the other body and saw lying next to it a familiar, worn leather fedora, and, although the dead man's face was obscured with blood, he knew at once who it was. He leaned down and knelt next to his dead brother.

"*Drop the gun and put your hands in the air!*"

The booming voice from behind sent a sharp chill up Jason's spine. *Damn it!* he thought, kicking himself for forgetting about the police. He let the pistol slide through his fingers and onto the floor and then slowly raised his hands.

"Now, stand up and turn around so I can see you," the voice said.

Jason did as he was told, and as he turned he was surprised to see only two men: one, about 5'7", wearing plain clothes, pointing a pistol at his face; the other, approximately 6'2", in uniform, wielding a shotgun.

The one in plain clothes was clearly in charge. He glanced around at the disaster that used to be a diner. "*Damn,* Roberts," he said. "I'd say this guy's one *mean* son-of-a-bitch."

Officer Roberts smiled and leveled his 12 gauge on Jason, cherishing the moment. Action like this was scarce in the Podunk 3rd Precinct, and it was a rare pleasure to aim a gun at a real person as opposed to a cardboard cutout. Wielding that kind of power made up for his deep lack of self-confidence, and the adrenaline rush felt really good.

"You went a little too far this time, my friend," he said.

Jason hated when strangers called him *friend* — especially cops. He looked at Roberts and his shotgun, weighing his options. "I'm not your friend," he said.

Roberts's eyes narrowed and his finger twitched on his shotgun's hair trigger.

"I'll need to see some I.D.," the man in charge said.

Jason wished he'd gotten around to changing the name on his driver's license to the pseudonym he used around Brandy: 'Jason Beckham'; but it was too late now, so he reluctantly handed the license over.

"*Jason Souther*," the one in plain clothes read aloud. "I'm Detective Harness, Third Precinct. This is Officer Roberts." He indicated his partner.

Jason did not respond. Not counting visiting rooms, he had never set foot inside a bonafide state prison, much less done time in one. Sure, he'd overnighted in a few county jails, and there were the three months in the brig awaiting his dishonorable discharge from the Navy; but whenever there'd been serious trouble, his big brother had always figured out a clever way to take the fall for him — spending half his life behind prison bars so that his little brother could remain free. Jason had always loved and respected Johnny for that.

But his big brother was dead now, and he couldn't take the fall for him this time. Jason was finally going to experience, first hand, what Johnny Souther had tried so hard, and for so long, to protect him from.

Always the teacher, Detective Harness looked at his partner. "Roberts," he said. "Pretend you're in charge. What would you do in this situation?"

Roberts's grin widened. He had always thought he *should* be the one in charge. "I'd waste this fucker right here, right now," he said, without hesitation.

Jason swallowed and glanced at Harness.

Harness returned Jason's glance. "I'm not sure I'd recommend that, Roberts. In case you missed that chapter in the handbook, police brutality is frowned upon in this city."

"No one would ever know," Roberts said, eyes widening at the thought. "Basic self-defense ... stands up in court like a dick on prom night."

Roberts's clever bits of humor always put a smile on Harness's face. That, and the fact that he was fearless, were why he had chosen Roberts as his partner in the first place.

Beads of cold sweat had formed on Jason's brow; his chances for escape were diminishing by the second. If he was going to make a move, he'd have to make it soon.

Out of the corner of his eye he saw his pistol lying on the floor, three feet from him, and, in spite of a serious adrenaline rush, he forced himself to stay calm.

"Cuff him," Harness said to Roberts. "And be quick about it. We have that fatal car crash to attend to. I'll meet you in the car."

"Yes, sir," Roberts said.

Harness turned to leave.

Roberts glanced down to pull two long, white zip-ties out of his equipment belt. Jason saw him, dove for his gun, rolled over, and fired, the bullet smacking Roberts square in the chest, sending him flying onto his back as his shotgun discharged harmlessly into the ceiling.

Harness wheeled around and fired, catching Jason in the thigh as he leaped to his feet. Jason tackled Harness, sending the two of them crashing over a table and onto the floor. Both pistols came loose.

Harness scrabbled for the shotgun, but Jason outweighed him by forty pounds, catching his arm as they rolled over again and again in a desperate struggle. At last Jason managed to grab a handful of Harness hair and slam his head into the chrome base of a barstool, knocking him unconscious.

Just then Harness's backup arrived in a blaze of flashing lights and deafening sirens.

Jason took one look, and then limped out the back door just as the front door exploded open.

Chapter 6

When Detective Harness came to, two uniformed officers were kneeling next to him. "Roberts?" he said, looking around. He tried to sit up, but the officers gently held him down.

"Officer Roberts is dead, sir," one said. "Please don't try to move."

Harness waved the officers off and sat up, his head pounding. He spotted Roberts lying motionless a few feet away. It was true: his partner, and long-time friend, had taken a bullet through his heart. He looked at the officers urgently. "The suspect," he said. "Where's *the suspect?*"

"He evaded us, sir."

"*What?*" Harness demanded. He glanced outside and saw the black Hummer still parked in front of the diner. "He's on foot and bleeding from a fucking gunshot wound to the leg! How the hell could he evade you?"

"We're sorry, sir. H-he was gone when we arrived. There's an APB out and at least three units are —"

"*FUCK!*" Harness shouted, pounding the floor with his fist. "*They're wasting their time!*" He got to his feet and looked around, disgusted with himself. "You've got this covered?" he said, indicating the crime scene.

"Yes, sir."

Harness headed for the door, throwing Roberts's body a quick salute on his way out.

Exiting the diner, Harness was blinded by the flashing lights of an ambulance parked halfway up on the sidewalk. Two harried paramedics, the oldest no more than twenty, were heading his way, pushing a heavy gurney. He stepped aside to avoid losing some toes.

He walked over to check out the black Hummer, noting that the front end was smashed in and there were fresh streaks of silver paint scraped into the chrome and down the right side.

He and Roberts had cruised by the accident scene on their way to the diner, and one look at the gruesome wreckage had told them three things: 1) It was a felony hit-and-run; 2) There were no survivors; and 3) The other vehicle had been big and heavy. Could it be he was standing next to the other vehicle?

He checked the glove box for the registration. The Hummer was registered in the name of Jason Souther.

I knew it! Harness thought miserably. He had had the guy in his grasp! The thought sickened him.

He shined his light around the vehicle's interior and was shocked to see a young boy, twelve or thirteen maybe, asleep on the back seat covered in a wool blanket. He quietly opened the rear side door and laid a gentle hand on the boy's leg, speaking softly.

"Kid ... are you all right?" he said.

Aaron jerked awake and tried to lift his head, but the pain was too great and all he could manage was a feeble groan through gritted teeth.

Harness lifted the blanket gently to see what he was dealing with: The boy looked bad, his face blackened and bloodied. Two purple gashes were obvious on the left side of his face: one, partially healed, across his upper left cheek bone, and a fresh laceration running vertically from there to his lower jaw line. But both had clotted over and could wait.

Harness opened Aaron's oddly oversized, black overcoat. It was damp and smelled like wet dog. Fresh blood seeped from a bandage in the area of his chest and shoulder. He closed the coat and replaced the blanket, and then he pulled his sleeve down over the heel of his hand and wiped some of the dirt and blood from Aaron's face.

He thought of Jason Souther, finding it hard to believe that a man would drive so recklessly with his child on board. If he ever married and had children of his own, he would never do that.

Sorry, kid, he thought sadly, *but if we ever catch up with him, your daddy's going to prison for a long, long time.*

Back in the diner, the officers were busy filling out a report. The two paramedics had zipped Officer Roberts and Johnny Souther up in fluid-tight body bags and were preparing to lift one of them onto the gurney.

Harness leaned out of the Hummer and called to them. "Hey kids!" he shouted. "Leave those poor bastards for the coroner. Trundle your butts out here and help the *living*."

The paramedics looked at each other then quickly followed the detective's orders.

Chapter 7

Harness stood by while the paramedics transferred Aaron onto the gurney and carefully strapped him down in preparation for loading into the ambulance.

Aaron was awake. He looked at Harness. "My mother," he said weakly. "I-is she okay?"

Your mother was with you? Harness thought, incredulous. He had assumed that the boy and his dad were the only passengers in the Hummer. He was about to ask Aaron to explain, when suddenly a clear image of the crash scene flashed into his mind and he made the connection. He'd been concentrating on the *wrong vehicle!*

"Wait a minute ..." he said. "You and your mom ... you were in the Aston Martin?"

Aaron nodded.

Oh my God, Harness thought. "I thought you were —" He glanced at the Hummer and stopped himself. This was too much to believe. "Was anyone else in the Aston with you?"

All hope drained from Aaron's face. He knew what was coming next. "Yes," he replied, "My best friend, Willy ... a- and my new dad, Michael."

Harness rested his hand on Aaron's shoulder. "What's your name, kid?"

"Aaron Quinn."

"I am so sorry, Aaron ... but I'd bet my badge that with the exception of the little miracle I see lying before me on this gurney, no one could possibly have survived that wreck."

Aaron closed his eyes and turned his head away. God had given him everything he'd wished for ... and now He'd taken it all away.

Harness took out one of his business cards and placed it in Aaron's hand. "My name's Jim," he said. "Call me anytime, for any reason, okay?"

Aaron nodded and closed his fingers over the card. Harness patted him on the arm, and the paramedics finished loading him into the ambulance.

"I want hourly updates on this kid's condition," Harness ordered. "You got that?"

"Yes, sir," one said.

Satisfied that the boy was in capable hands, Harness took the patrol car and drove back over to the scene of the accident.

Chapter 8

Brandy Fine sat in Jason's apartment staring at a blank TV screen. She heard a car pull up and ran to the window, but there was no black Hummer, just another taxi cab. But then she saw Jason Beckham step out and pay the driver.

That's odd, she thought. She could have sworn Jason left in his Hummer. As she watched him enter the building she noticed he was limping. She quickly sat down and pretended she wasn't waiting for him.

The front door banged open. "Pack your bags," Jason barked. "We're leaving town." He grabbed Brandy's coat off a chair and tossed it to her.

Brandy was alarmed to see that one of his pant legs was soaked with blood; but before she could say anything, he snatched her car keys off the kitchen counter and limped out the door.

"What about Johnny?" she called after him, fumbling with the sleeves of her coat, her mind a blur.

"Johnny's dead," Jason said over his shoulder, his voice echoing in the wooden stairwell.

"*What?*" she said, closing the door behind her. "Oh, my God!" Then she stumbled down the hall after him.

Chapter 9

Jason had no way of knowing it at the time, but as he was backing his Hummer away from the dumpster back at the crash scene, he had come within inches of hitting a woman lying just to one side amid a pile of cardboard boxes. She was unconscious , but alive, thrown clear of the Aston Martin upon impact, just as her son had been.

Ashley came to and looked around, confused, unable to determine where she was or why she was there. Near her, smashed across the sidewalk, was a twisted, gray, street-light pole, its glass lens shattered and bulb burst — in the gloom it looked to Ashley like a great serpent that had suddenly turned to stone.

A light rain was falling and it was very cold. A sour, smoky odor burned her nostrils and she sensed that something horrible had happened, but she had no clue what it was.

She shoved some loose boxes aside and got to her feet, noticing that the bodice of her dress had been torn away in the area of her right breast, revealing one of the white-lace cups of her bra. She instinctively pulled her lavender, faux-suede jacket closed to cover herself.

Her head hurt, and when she put her hand to her forehead she touched what felt like streaks of dried mud, or perhaps blood. She thought of checking herself in her compact mirror, but her purse was nowhere to be found. She felt for her glasses, but they were missing too.

She looked down at her throbbing left calf and saw she had a deep gash, just below the hem of her sundress — it, too, had clotted over, and she knew she'd been unconscious for quite a while.

She started when she saw flashing lights and several men in uniform hovering around what appeared to be the smoldering wreckage of a car in the middle of the street. The area had been cordoned off from the public with wide, yellow plastic tape with the familiar phrase:

POLICE - Do Not Cross — POLICE - Do Not Cross.

The car's fabric top had burned away, exposing its skeletal frame, and under the receding coating of fire-extinguishing foam, the car lay blackened and cold, like the ravaged corpse of a mastodon after an arctic thaw.

A midnight blue van was parked nearby, the word CORONER painted in bright yellow on its side; but it meant nothing to her. She felt no anguish, no emotion of any kind, only a deep, overwhelming sense of numbness.

Detective Harness pulled up to the scene in his cruiser. He stepped out and shook hands with some of the men and then stepped over to inspect the charred remains of the Aston Martin.

The vehicle lay on its side and was totaled, but Harness found enough of the original paint to verify that it had indeed been tungsten silver — a stock color for the DBS during that model year, and the same shade as the paint he'd found on the Hummer. He followed two faint skid marks up the street and found a small piece of amber turn-signal lens — a tiny, but vital clue that would no doubt fit nicely into the front-left lighting cluster of that same black Hummer.

Ashley watched from the shadows. She felt no need to call to the men as they went about their work. She felt nothing, wanting nothing. She was very tired, but she no longer knew why. A lot had happened to her in the last 72 hours, but she remembered none of it.

She discovered she was clutching something in her left hand. It was the photo Aaron had given her just before the accident, the photo of her with Aaron's father, Danny, in the alpine meadow. But Ashley didn't recognize it. She had no idea where the snapshot came from or who the man she was hugging in the photo was.

She absently tucked the photo into her jacket pocket and wandered off down the street.

Detective Harness walked the area's perimeter searching for more clues. He came to the downed light pole and saw the evidence of a car having smashed through it and into a nearby dumpster. But there was no car.

Near the dumpster he was surprised to find a woman's purse partially covered by a loose cardboard box. The purse was cheap vinyl but new. He checked inside: a hair brush, a bottle of acetaminophen 500s, a set of car keys, a small cell phone, and a credit card. The name on the credit card read:

Ashley Quinn

Harness did a double-take. The purse belonged to the boy's *mother!*

He quickly checked the immediate area, hoping to find Ashley alive. But she was nowhere to be found and he had to assume she had died in the crash.

He stopped when he spotted a small fragment of cloth lying on the sidewalk. It was wet from the rain, but appeared to be printed cotton, a fabric commonly used in a woman's dress, and it was *new*. He glanced back at the wreckage, judging the distance at thirty feet, and wondered how a piece of light fabric could have been thrown that far.

Then something shiny caught his eye. It was a pair of women's eyeglasses. They were shattered and bent, but the frames were certainly newer than the other trash in the gutter. He tucked the glasses and the piece of fabric into a plastic bag with the other evidence.

When he had concluded his search, Harness climbed into his cruiser and left the scene, knowing he — and whoever his new partner turned out to be — had a nearly impossible task ahead of them.

~ PART I ~

WEDNESDAY
TWO YEARS LATER ...

VLADIVOSTOK, RUSSIA

Chapter 10

Captain Second Rank (Ret.) Vtorak Borisovich Pankov washed the last bite of his potato omelet down with coffee and wiped his mouth with his napkin. He carefully folded his copy of this morning's *Moscow Times* and looked at the two men seated across the table from him.

"So," he said. "You were able to make a deal?"

Uri Ruden, Pankov's long-time friend and confidant slid some papers forward. "The agents from the American government have signed the necessary paperwork, Captain. Congratulations. B-39, Cobra, is yours, once again."

"So, you are aware that she was my former command," Pankov said, leafing through the documents.

Uri winced. Clearly his old friend's mind was not as sharp as it used to be. Must he constantly remind Pankov that he, too, was a retired Soviet submariner, a Captain Third Rank, who had served under Pankov on Cobra during the Cold War Seventies and early Eighties? Out of respect for the legendary captain, Uri restrained himself. "But of course, Captain, your exemplary command of Cobra is well documented. You spent your entire military career in the Soviet Submarine Service — as did I, sir."

"The Soviet Submarine Service," Pankov said, pausing to reflect. "The hand-picked elite of the Soviet Navy."

"Yes, sir," Uri said.

Pankov turned to their guest, Commander Richard Fagan, 38, a highly decorated, active duty submariner with the United States Navy.

"Cobra and I sailed the world together, you know," Pankov said, "from right here in her home port of Vladivostok, Russia."

Commander Fagan smiled. "It's rumored that during your last mission you had the skill and audacity to navigate her into San Francisco Bay in broad daylight, passing under the Golden Gate Bridge and circumnavigating Alcatraz Island."

Pankov's eyes brightened at that memory. "All true," he said. "We could have neutralized half of California with the nuclear arsenal we carried."

He paused, the smile fading from his expression.

"But while my torpedoes collected dust, Brezhnev and his 'collective leadership' thought it best to play pointless *games* with the Imperialist United States."

"A complete waste of time, in my opinion, sir," Fagan said. As a history buff he was enjoying this journey back through time. "And we can't forget the Cuban Missile Crisis."

"Ah, yes," Pankov said. "The 'Incident in Cuba', as you Americans like to call it."

"If I have my facts straight," Fagan said, "you were the spearhead of an effort to develop a Soviet naval base at Mariel Bay, there in Cuba."

"I remember it like it was yesterday," Pankov said. "27 October, 1962. Our submarines had been patrolling the area for weeks. Suddenly the U.S. naval destroyers start lobbing Practice Depth Charges at us to induce us to surface and identify ourselves. Of course, after weeks undersea in difficult circumstances, we were totally exhausted, and we had no way of knowing that the PDCs were anything less than *highly dangerous explosives*. And, to make matters worse, we were unable to establish communications with Moscow."

"You've got to be kidding me," Fagan said.

"Kennedy and McNamara were overreacting, as usual, treating us like children," Pankov went on. "The idiots had no idea that each of the submarines they were harassing carried a torpedo with a nuclear warhead whose fifteen kiloton explosive yield approximated the bomb that hit Hiroshima in 1945. Several of our submarines did finally exhaust their batteries, forcing them to surface, but b-39, Cobra, stayed down — and Kennedy and his men didn't know it." He paused to take a sip of ice water. "I was so tired and angry I ordered my nuclear torpedo to be assembled for battle readiness. 'We're going to blast them!' I told my officers. 'We will most certainly die, but we will sink them all before we go!' I remember my security officer staring at me and then fainting dead!"

Fagan was dumbfounded. How could he become a high-ranking U.S. Naval Officer and not have heard about this?

"The citizens of the United States never knew it, Commander," Pankov said, "but I, Captain Vtorak Borisovich Pankov, came this close to starting World War III." He held his thumb and forefinger up about a quarter-inch apart. "The biggest regret of my life is that I let my deputy brigade commander talk me out of it!"

Fagan paused as the enormity of Pankov's words sunk in. "Fascinating, sir," he said at last. "I had no idea we came that close to nuclear Armageddon."

"Were it not for a critical lack of bold leadership," Pankov said, "the Soviet Navy could easily have overwhelmed the Americans, rendering their nuclear options moot. Left to our own devices, the Soviet Submarine Service most certainly would have prevented the eventual collapse of the Soviet Union!"

Uri Ruden wholeheartedly agreed, but he needed to get the conversation back on the business at hand. "You are correct, sir. That period in our country's history was terribly frustrating for every Soviet submariner. But you must be pleased and proud to be taking command of your beloved b-39 once again."

Pankov's smile returned and he placed his hand on Uri's shoulder. "I *am* pleased, Uri, very pleased indeed. I never thought I would see the day."

"I'm pleased as well, Captain," Uri said.

Chapter 11

The waiter cleared Pankov's plate and refilled his coffee. Pankov took a big sip and gazed out the window overlooking Vladivostok Harbor.

"When, exactly, may I take command of Cobra?" Pankov asked.

"She's ready now, sir," Uri said.

Pankov considered for a moment. "That is good to know," he said. "How many years has it been?"

Uri suddenly found himself on the defensive. Six years sounds like a long time, unless, of course, you're the one doing all the work. He took a sip of water before answering.

"It took six years, Captain," he said. "As you can imagine, purchasing a functioning Russian attack submarine and relocating it to a foreign country is an extremely complex task, requiring the cooperation of many people — many loyal, high-level people."

"I can appreciate that, Uri," Pankov said.

"After leaving Vladivostok Harbor," Uri went on, "Cobra set sail for Finland for light repairs, then all the way to Vancouver, B.C., followed by a full restoration in Seattle before arriving, as you requested, at her final destination on the waterfront of San Diego Bay — where she is hiding in plain sight as part of the Maritime Museum of San Diego."

He gestured toward Commander Fagan. "And thanks to the expertise and resourcefulness of our esteemed colleague, all went exactly as planned."

"Thank you, Uri," Fagan said, nodding his appreciation. "And thank you for your impressive efforts, as well." He turned to Pankov. "I have one concern, Captain. Uri tells me we'll be running a skeleton crew."

"That is correct," Pankov said.

"How many men would you say? Forty? Fifty?"

"We'll be running three, Commander," Pankov said frankly. "Myself, Captain Ruden, and you."

Piloting an attack submarine with three men? Fagan thought. It was insane to even consider it.

"With all due respect, sir," he said, "I seriously doubt that the three of us could pull it off. A submarine in Cobra's class normally requires a crew of seventy-eight, including a dozen or more officers."

Uri Ruden stepped in on Pankov's behalf. "We'll be submerged for less than an hour. Traveling ten to fifteen nautical miles maximum. We can do without many non-essential crew."

"Such as?" Fagan said.

"Well," Uri said, "to name a few ... we won't need a navigator or assistant navigator, a torpedo officer and his assistant and crew, or an electronics officer for sonar, radar, and radio. We'll be relying on the available air, so we won't have to worry about oxygen, and we can do without a mechanical engineer and his assistants, and a duty officer. I'm sure you can come up with a list of your own if you think about it."

"It would be very tight," Fagan said. "If not impossible."

"In order to run quiet we won't be powering up the diesels," Uri said. "We will charge the batteries before we leave, and with the exception of engaging the drives, the electric motors practically run themselves."

Fagan knew he was losing the argument and decided the time had come to show his hand. "Uri, as your friend and as U.S. military consultant for the mission, I would strongly recommend we have at least one other experienced submarine officer on board."

Uri paused. "Let's say I agree with you, Richard. It will be exceedingly difficult to find someone we can trust. Someone who hates the United States as much we do. Someone who is not only a qualified submariner but also experienced with diesel-electrics like b-39."

I don't hate the United States, Uri, Fagan thought. *I just hate the President.*

"Are you prepared to recommend someone with these qualifications, Commander?" Pankov said. "Right now? At this table? At this late date?"

"I am indeed, sir," Fagan said confidently. He removed a navy-blue, leather-bound dossier from his briefcase and placed it on the table. "I was about to recommend this man in any case."

He calmly slid the dossier toward Pankov, thanking himself for coming to the meeting fully prepared.

Pankov opened the dossier and found the name printed at the top of the resume. It read:

JASON SOUTHER

"I'll be the first to admit it, sir, he's a bit of a maverick," Fagan said. "But he's brilliant ... and as fine a submariner as you could ask for — maybe the best America's ever seen. He served under me for three years in San Diego, at Naval Base Point Loma, right up until his discharge."

"A dishonorable discharge, I see," Pankov remarked.

"I can explain that, sir." Fagan said. "Jason's brother Johnny got sent up for armed robbery, and, well, I guess he was having a difficult time getting along with some of the other prisoners. In other words, his life was in serious danger. Jason thought if he could pay him a quick visit, he could help him out somehow. So he requested a one-day leave, you know, to visit San Quentin, but the Navy refused him. So he went AWOL for a day, and the Navy didn't appreciate it, and when he returned from San Francisco he was arrested."

Pankov nodded and read on. "It says here he is wanted for the murder of a police officer, and for multiple counts of felony hit-and-run manslaughter."

"That is correct, Captain," Fagan said. "He's also single, and fearless. I already mentioned brilliant. And he hates the United States as much as you do."

"Because of the dishonorable discharge?" Pankov asked.

"Among other things," Fagan said. "After his discharge, Jason went a little crazy, and he was only home with his wife for a few days before he took off again without a word. As you well know, the life of a military wife is tough enough, considering her man is gone all the time, and combined with the shame of her husband's dishonorable discharge and the painful gossip and finger-pointing among the closely knit social group of Navy wives, Jason's sudden disappearance was too much for her. She couldn't handle it. So she committed suicide. And, well, Jason never forgave himself, and he blames his country for what happened. All because he asked for a one-day leave to visit his brother."

Pankov showed no emotion and turned the page. "It says here 'current whereabouts unknown'. Are you certain you can find him?"

"I already have," Fagan replied. "My sources have him living in the Caribbean — on Grand Cayman in the Cayman Islands to be precise — and I can fly down there tomorrow to talk with him. I've known Jason Souther a long time, Captain, and I believe I can persuade him to meet with us."

Pankov closed the dossier and folded his hands comfortably in front of him. "Uri Ruden has known you for a long time, Commander. I trust his judgment — and in turn I trust yours. How soon can we meet him?"

"Soon, sir. I don't want to give him time to talk himself out of it," Fagan said. "I know you had hoped to make a preliminary visit to San Diego soon, and I know how much you like omelets, so I've reserved us a table for this Sunday, for brunch, at the Hotel Del Coronado, on Coronado Island."

"I've heard of it," Pankov said. "The oldest hotel in the United States. Amazing Victorian architecture. Several U.S. Presidents have stayed there."

"They have the best omelets on earth," Fagan said, "and after the meeting we can take a tour of b-39 in her new berth at MMSD, just to the north, across San Diego Bay."

Pankov leaned back in his chair and checked his watch. 11:00 a.m. Vladivostok Time. "It is agreed. We shall meet with your friend. If you can persuade him to meet with us, that is."

"I trust you will offer to pay him, Captain?" Fagan said.

"Of course," Pankov said. "Many important people in Russia are counting on our success, and to them this mission is considered critical. They are prepared to offer a considerable reward — to us, and anyone we choose to help us."

"Considerable, sir?" Fagan said. "We'll be asking a lot of this man."

"Suffice it to say, if your friend agrees to help us, he will never work another day in his life," Pankov said.

He stood, followed by Uri and Fagan, and they shook hands across the table.

"For the good of the People!" Pankov said.

"For the good of the People, sir!" Uri said.

"Party, People, and Nation!" Pankov said.

"Party, People, and Nation, sir!" Uri said.

Uri told Commander Fagan to go on ahead. Fagan nodded, and then excused himself and left the room.

Uri turned to Pankov. "Do you think we should have told him, Captain?"

Pankov was thinking the same thing and had his answer at hand. "I think it is best we leave well enough alone."

Uri nodded and stepped away from the table. "Is there anything else, Captain?" he said.

"Thank you, Uri," Pankov said. "That will be all."

Uri bowed slightly. "I will show myself out." He started for the door; then turned back and said, "It will be a pleasure sailing with you again, Captain. What we are planning to do ... it is grand."

"It is very grand indeed, Uri," Pankov replied. "Cobra is finally going to do what she was designed to do."

Chapter 12

Detective James Harness sat in his office back at police headquarters attempting to climb a mountain of paperwork.

He heard a knock at the door. "It's open," he said.

His new partner, Officer Larry Holt, ducked his head in. "You wanted to see me, sir?"

"Yes — come in, Holt," Harness said warmly. "Have a seat." Harness had taken it hard when his partner was gunned down two years earlier, and had resisted replacing him — that is until a week-and-a-half ago, when he met Larry Holt. Big and black and tough as asphalt, yet with a spark of intelligence in his eye, Holt was the first man Harness had met who had a fighting chance of filling Officer Roberts's sizable shoes. Harness had recruited him on the spot.

Holt sat down on the worn sofa that filled half of Harness's office. The cushions had long since collapsed and Holt was so big and sat so low he had to look between his knees to see Harness's face.

Harness reached for a file folder, kicked off his shoes, and leaned back in his chair, resting his stocking feet on the desk.

"You remember that guy I told you about? Jason Souther?" Harness said, opening the folder.

"The one you been after for two years," Holt said. "Killed that family in that hit-'n-run and then killed that dude in the diner before he shot your —" Holt was about to say *partner* but caught himself.

"It's okay, Holt," Harness said. "Roberts was a good man, but I've moved on. Regarding Jason Souther, however ... It's becoming obvious that I've exhausted all of my leads here in the U.S., and, well, I've heard vague rumblings about a guy fitting Jason's description being spotted somewhere in the Caribbean."

Holt knew where this was going and didn't like it.

"I know it's crazy," Harness said, "and a total long shot, but I think I may have to go international."

Holt was deeply hurt. He'd been Detective Harnesses's partner for almost two weeks now, and he liked the way it made him feel. It was a big promotion for him, an accomplishment of which he was very proud. But somewhere deep inside he had known it was too good to be true, and he was glad he had put off sharing his good fortune with his wife and young daughter.

"Let's say you did take your search international," Holt said at last. "You'd have to quit the force, right?"

Harness paused. "I know what you're thinking, Holt, and I'm well aware of the rules concerning international fugitives. But if it comes to that ... then yes, I may have to quit the force. But I'd certainly put in for a leave of absence first, and —"

"Cool. For how long?"

"I don't know, six weeks — two months maybe," Harness said. Then he paused for a moment. "Listen, I know I may be working outside the law, but I have no choice, okay? This son-of-a-bitch has been eating my insides out for two long years, and I can't just let him run free. I have to go after him."

"Let's say they gave you the LOA," Holt said. "You really don't know how long you'll be gone. What are you gonna do for transportation and lodging? Stow away on a fucking steamer? Think about it, sir. Chasin' some mystic motherfucker around the world ain't gonna be cheap."

Harness hadn't really thought about the amount of cash his vendetta might require. But logistics were *his* problem not Holt's. "What's this got to do with you, anyway?" he said coldly.

It was obvious to Holt that his partner had little concern for how this affected *him*. "If you want the truth, sir," he said. "I think you're outa your damn mind."

Harness closed Jason's file and sat up in his chair. He didn't have to take crap from a subordinate, even if he *was* his partner. "You know what I think, Holt? I think you should go find a quiet place and fuck yourself."

Holt stood up from the sofa. "Glad I could help, sir," he said and started for the door.

"I don't *need* your help," Harness barked after him, "or anyone else's. You got that?"

Holt paused in the doorway, his back to Detective Harness. "So, I guess this means I ain't going with you."

Harness hesitated, surprised. "What are you talking about? You weren't thinking about *joining* me in this insanity ..."

Holt kept his back turned and said nothing.

"If headquarters finds out what we're up to, it'll be the end of *both* our careers," Harness said.

Holt remained quiet.

"We could die, Holt ... or worse. Jason Souther's as cold-blooded as they come."

Holt turned and looked at Harness. "Cut the bullshit, Detective. I'm a damn good cop, okay? And this may come as a shock to you, but I have some money saved. Why not just get the hell outa your own way and let me help you *find* this asshole? Am I your damn partner or ain't I?"

Harness looked at him, feeling foolish. He had seriously underestimated his new recruit. Who knew an officer as green as Holt could be so loyal, willing to risk everything for his partner's irrational vendetta, a mission that would likely collapse into a career-ending fiasco?

He stood and gave Holt's huge hand a firm two-handed shake. "My sincerest apologies, Officer Holt. Welcome to my nightmare."

GRAND CAYMAN

Chapter 13

Jason Souther pulled an old lawn chair up to the starboard railing of his run-down 24-foot cabin-cruiser and sat down, shading his gray eyes from the intensity of the western Caribbean sun. He had been tracking the *Cayman Jewel,* a foreign tourist's 65-foot, custom motor yacht since early that morning, and when, at long last, the man had set anchor, Jason had anchored as well, at a safe distance of nearly half a mile.

He surveyed the luxury yacht through a pair of high-powered binoculars. The only man aboard moved about the boat dressed in a white robe, and judging by the two young women lounging on deck in bikinis Jason had a pretty good idea what was coming next.

"Keep her on this heading," Jason called to the wheelhouse.

Even though they were safely anchored, Brandy Fine got excited whenever Jason let her take the helm. But after two years in the Caymans she'd grown tired of living aboard a dilapidated tub, and what Jason was preparing to do excited her even more. "Aye aye, Captain," she replied.

Jason turned his gaze toward shore. They were barely within sight of the small Cayman Island town of Grand Cayman, the town they called home. The skies were clear and the seas dead calm. Conditions were perfect.

He folded a clean white towel over the railing and gently nestled the barrel of his new Accuracy International AWSM

.338 Lapua Magnum sniper rifle into the soft terry padding. Then he put his eye to the powerful 10x42 telescopic sight.

Jason had learned to handle a sniper rifle during his stint in the Navy (his friends in the Army used to kid him about being a sniper on a submarine) and although the target was over half a mile away, in the hands of an expert marksman it was easily within the AWSM's effective range.

He dialed in the scope and spotted an unopened bottle of Domaine de la Romanée-Conti (vintage 1997) on a silver tray next to one of the girls. It seemed a shame to waste such an expensive bottle of wine, so Jason made a mental note to share it with Brandy later.

He had killed twice before: once when he was helping Johnny pull one of his bank jobs and a guard got too frisky; and more recently the cop with the shotgun back at Sally's Diner.

Jason didn't enjoy killing — had even thrown up once, after the incident with the bank guard. But the money was all gone, and sometimes a man must do what a man must do. He wiped the sweat off his brow with the back of his hand then returned his attention to the *Cayman Jewel*.

The girls were obviously having a great time, the sun warming their skin, their hair blowing in the soft tropical breeze. One appeared to look in Jason's direction, but he knew that at over 1,500 yards, his little cabin-cruiser would be a mere pimple on the horizon.

The man came into view carrying a tray of drinks. He approached his lady friends and took a seat between them. After a quick toast, the girls wasted no time getting the party started, and in the blink of an eye, the only thing they were wearing were their diamonds.

Jason smiled. After months of struggle, botched attempts, and several close calls, he had begun to doubt the wisdom of his decision to try pirating for a living. But now, with the tactical advantage of his new sniper rifle, his luck was about to change.

He waited until the man's sunscreen-caked forehead was centered in his crosshairs, and then he slowly squeezed the trigger.

POP!

The top third of the man's head disappeared in a puff of red mist, spitting bits of brain and bone on the girls and their diamonds. To their infinite horror, the man remained conscious long enough to look into their eyes — as if to say, *What the fuck just happened?*

Jason watched through his scope as the body slumped forward and rolled onto the deck. The girls screamed — distant, silent screams — and looked around, mortified, clutching white beach towels to their soiled breasts.

Jason smiled, proud of his marksmanship. He preferred killing at a distance. Watching someone die through the scope was like watching it on a movie screen — it was unreal, surreal even, and much easier on the stomach.

Today would be a good day — a very good day. At last, for him and for Brandy, things were about to change. The beautiful, 65-foot *Cayman Jewel* and all of its bounty would soon be theirs, carrying with the distinct, if not dubious, honor of being their ticket out of poverty.

Brandy heard the pop of the rifle's suppressor and poked her head out of the wheel house. "Well?" she said. "You spent our last dollar on that damn rifle ... did it work?"

"Of course it worked," Jason said, carefully wiping his expensive rifle down with the towel to remove any salt spray.

"I can't believe the range it has," Brandy said. "I couldn't even see the *boat,* much less the target."

"The AWSM is rated at over 1,600 yards," Jason said. "Back in 2009, in Afghanistan, a UK sniper used the same rifle to hit two enemy machine gunners consecutively at a range of 2,707 yards. That's over a mile and a half. Longest kill on record."

"Unbelievable," Brandy said.

"I'll take the helm now," Jason said, returning the rifle to its case. "Put on something sexy. You're going to look really good in diamonds."

Chapter 14

Jason maneuvered his boat up next to the *Cayman Jewel*. Brandy tossed two dock fenders over the side, and Jason tied up toward the *Jewel's* stern near her swim step where she was lower to the water and they could more easily board.

He instructed Brandy to stay behind and stand ready to untie if necessary; then he pulled his pistol and stepped aboard their new yacht.

Jason had been on some nice boats before but never one as nice at this. The exquisite luxury yacht felt huge when compared with his, and exquisite in every detail. If ever a king's palace could float, this would be it.

The dead man lay face down in a pool of blood that had soaked into the teak decking. Jason kicked himself for not doing the deed when the man was over an area decked with fiberglass — this was going to be difficult to clean.

The girls were nowhere to be seen. Jason walked every inch of the upper decks and then headed downstairs to check below.

Having checked every conceivable hiding place, Jason found no one. He made his way topside and looked back across the water toward Grand Cayman. Only an experienced ocean swimmer could reach shore from this far out, and after seeing how they were built, Jason knew these girls didn't qualify. He spotted one of the white beach towels floating nearby and his suspicion was confirmed: The girls had chosen drowning over the horror of ending up like their boyfriend, basically committing suicide.

Jason weighted the body with some SCUBA weights and several yards of duct tape, and then tossed it overboard. He did a cursory cleaning and covered the remaining bloodstains with a clean towel — as he had expected, a thorough scrubbing was required. Then he jumped back over onto his old cabin-cruiser.

"Pack your things," he said to Brandy.

"Really?" Brandy said. She kissed Jason on the cheek and touched her hand on her throat as if she were already wearing her new diamond necklace.

Jason saw this and said, "You can forget about the jewelry. The girls jumped overboard, taking their diamonds with them."

"*What?* You're kidding me!"

"With a million in diamonds weighing them down, they'd have sunk like stones. It all belongs to Davy Jones now."

Brandy touched her fingers to her throat again and a tear rolled down her cheek.

Jason and Brandy abandoned their old boat and boarded the new one. Jason untied and set the cabin-cruiser adrift.

In spite of their losses, Jason and Brandy had plenty to celebrate. After all, the *Cayman Jewel* was worth ten times what the diamonds would have brought. Jason poured two glasses of Dom. Romane Conti, and he and Brandy toasted their success.

"I'm really sorry about the diamonds," Jason said, stroking her hair.

Brandy was touched. Jason hadn't appeared to care one way or the other. A million in diamonds would have suited her just fine, but she was content in their new home. "I'll live," she said, managing a little smile.

They finished the first bottle of wine and as Jason went to open another, Brandy took him by the arm and led him below decks to thank him for her new yacht.

Chapter 15

When Jason awoke the next day, it took a moment for his confusion to clear. Then he remembered he was aboard the *Cayman Jewel*.

He climbed out of bed and looked out the cabin's large tinted window. The sun was nearly overhead.

He hadn't slept much the night before. His plan to steal the luxury yacht had gone well, of course, but not *that* well. His chances of selling the yacht without getting caught were slim to none, and the diamonds he was counting on to raise some cash had gone to the bottom of the sea. How would they pay for fuel and maintenance — and food? How would they live?

He felt an urgent need to get off the yacht and go ashore for a while. He picked his jeans up off a chair and pulled what remaining cash he had out of the pocket: forty U.S. dollars — enough for one good lunch.

He reached over and shook Brandy awake. "Wake up," he said. "We're going out to eat."

Brandy raised her head and aimed one sleepy eye at the clock, and then flopped back down on the pillow. "It's *too early* ..." she whined.

"It's 12:30," Jason said. "Get dressed, I'm hungry."

Brandy talked Jason into letting her take a quick shower, and then they went to lunch at a popular Grand Cayman, beach-front, burger restaurant.

The hostess seated them at a table by the water and their server took their drink and appetizer orders.

Jason had planned to talk to Brandy about their need for cash; but before he could get a word out, Brandy held her left hand out to him and wiggled her naked ring finger. "See this," she said. "It's been two years since you hauled me down here to the Caymans, and it's still bare!"

This was the last thing on Jason's mind and he couldn't come up with a good answer. "I said I'd marry you and I will," he said bluntly.

"You've told me that like a *million* times!" Brandy cried. "I'm growing *old* listening to your excuses."

Even though they couldn't afford their new yacht, Jason figured it still carried some weight in an argument. "I got you a new yacht, didn't I? That should count for *something*."

That statement was so utterly ridiculous, Brandy couldn't even laugh. She held up her hands, shaking her head. "Whatever." Then she turned to look out at the water.

She noticed a young man sitting in the booth next to them. He wore a ball cap pulled down over shoulder length, sun-bleached brown hair. She guessed he was eighteen or nineteen. The young man's back was turned and he continued to work on a green-chili burger with no onions and no cheese. He had sailed 80 miles down to Grand Cayman from his home in Cayman Brac just for this meal, and he was savoring every morsel, washing each delicious bite down with a sip from a double Jack Daniel's on the rocks.

"Excuse me," Brandy said, tapping him on the shoulder.

The young man started and turned toward her. The stitching on his cap read, *Tortuga Golden Original Rum Cake*.

"Would you like to get married?" she asked.

This caught the young man like a well-placed right hook, and he was struck mute.

Brandy looked back at Jason, as if to say, *Take that, you bastard. If you won't give me what I want, I'll find someone who will, damn it!*

After two years living together, Jason was no longer surprised by Brandy's antics, but this childishly random marriage proposal irritated him. He gave her a look that left no doubt as to his displeasure.

"Just kidding," she said, giving him a wry smile.

The young man felt foolish and returned to his burger.

Brandy leaned over and tapped him on the shoulder again. "I'm Brandy Fine," she said, offering him her hand. "And you are?"

The young man coughed and took a sip of water then looked back at Brandy. She was beautiful, in an exotic kind of way, with long, flowing red hair, and a great little body, and he didn't mind that she was probably ten or fifteen years older than he. However, she was obviously with someone, and for that reason she made him feel very uncomfortable.

"Uh — I'm Aaron Quinn," he replied, returning her handshake. Her skin felt warm and soft to the touch, and he was certain her lips would as well.

Brandy saw that Aaron had a scar running down the left side of his face but it only added to his rugged, yet youthful charm. "This is Jason Beckham," she said, cocking her head toward him.

The two men looked vaguely familiar to each other, but neither could pin down the reason, so they shook hands and let it go.

"Why don't you join us, Aaron?" Brandy said.

Aaron hesitated — he was content being alone, and all he really wanted to do was finish his burger.

Brandy patted the red-vinyl seat cushion next to her. "Come on. It's silly to make you talk over your shoulder."

Aaron glanced at Jason, thinking, *Are you down with where this is going?* Surprisingly, Jason showed no hostility toward him.

Aaron gathered up his lunch, and when he stood and came over to join them, Brandy's eyes went wide. He wore nothing but the cap, board shorts, and sandals, and at 5'10", 165 pounds, tanned, and ripped, Aaron looked amazing.

She wanted to reach out and touch him, but she restrained herself and scooted over to make room for him. He slid in next to her, and she felt a little dizzy. Her impromptu marriage proposal was sounding better by the second.

Jason saw her drooling and broke the spell. "We've ordered a pitcher of beer," he said to Aaron. "You want a glass?"

"Sounds good," Aaron replied. He preferred whiskey over beer, but he thought it would be rude to turn down Jason's offer.

Jason flagged down their server and asked for another glass, and when the beer and appetizers came, the three sat and enjoyed the food and the warm breezes coming off the Caribbean Sea.

"You look familiar, Aaron," Jason said, still trying to put a place with the face. "Do you live here in the Caymans?"

"I do," Aaron replied. "Up on Cayman Brac, on the beach near Earl's Reef Dive Shop. I'm a SCUBA instructor there. How about you guys? You from around here?"

"We're originally from the States," Jason said. "But for the last two years we've been living here on Grand Cayman aboard our boat." He pointed out a large yacht moored in the marina just west of the restaurant. "There on the end, with the black windows and maroon canvases."

Aaron followed Jason's gaze to the biggest yacht in the marina. "The *Cayman Jewel*?" he asked, surprised. She was more impressive than Aaron had expected — considering the casual appearance of its owners.

"That's her," Jason said.

"I don't remember seeing her here in Grand Cayman before."

Jason had to think fast. He hadn't had a chance to explain his new acquisition to anyone yet. "We just got her," he said at last.

"She certainly is beautiful," Aaron said. He pointed to a small sailboat rammed up on the beach near the restaurant. "That's my transpo, there."

Brandy could see the tiny craft leaning over on the sand. "You sailed all the way from Cayman Brac *in that*? That's like seventy or eighty miles. You must be one hell of a sailor."

Aaron blushed. It was true: After two years in the Caymans he'd become an expert sailor, but no one had ever pointed it out before. "I'm from the States, as well," he said, changing the subject.

"Why did you leave?" Brandy asked.

"Two years ago I was in a bad accident, and I was basically homeless," Aaron explained. "I didn't tell the hospital that, of course. I was only thirteen at the time and they would never have let me go."

You're only fifteen? Brandy thought, having done the math. She wasn't sure if that would change things for her or not, and decided it didn't.

"Where are your parents?" she asked.

"My parents are dead," Aaron said quickly, not wanting to go there. "I was living in a shelter down at the harbor near where this old fish cannery had been, and I ran into this wealthy retired couple who mentioned they were planning to sail their private yacht from Connecticut down to the Cayman Islands.

"It was pretty obvious that I was a homeless orphan, and why they didn't call Child Protective Services on me I'll never know. But I thank God they didn't, because instead they took pity on me and told me they could use an extra hand on the trip. I told them I had no sailing experience, but they didn't care. Long story short, my first hot meal and shower in months were in New Haven Harbor, aboard their yacht, and after smuggling me out of the country in a life-vest compartment we sailed down to the Caymans and I fell in love with the place and never left."

"I know the feeling," Jason mused.

"So I guess I've been here two years myself," Aaron calculated.

"You mentioned you were a diving instructor," Brandy said. "That sounds fascinating."

"Yeah, unlike back in the States, here in the Caymans you don't have to be fully certified to dive," Aaron said. "I can teach a beginner in under an hour — with the exception of wreck diving, that is. You have to be wreck certified to enter the interior of a wreck. No one wants to see an untrained tourist get stuck deep under water inside a sunken ship, in the dark, with no air, and no apparent way out."

Brandy stared at him, picturing herself in that predicament. "That would be awful!"

"And fatal," Jason added, grimly. He didn't want Brandy to get any ideas about taking SCUBA lessons.

"Diving is magical," Aaron said, returning to the lighter side. "It's one reason why people from around the world travel here to the Caymans."

"I've heard it's like flying," Brandy said with a sexy lilt in her voice.

"A submarine gives you a similar feeling," Jason said. "Except for the fact that you're packed inside a pressurized hull with a hundred other men, of course."

"You've been on a sub?" Aaron asked.

"You could say that," Jason replied smugly. "I'm a former submariner, a lieutenant commander with United States Navy."

"No kidding," Aaron said.

"I was stationed at Naval Base Point Loma, in San Diego, piloting nuclear submarines capable of sailing under the poles and staying down for months. I spent more time submerged than I did on dry land."

Aaron paused at the mention of San Diego. Before his father died, he had often overheard his parents talking about vacationing there together as a family. But he knew that that was never going to happen, so he returned his thoughts to the subject of submarines.

"I read somewhere that many foreign countries have started buying up old diesel-electrics," he said. "They can run on battery power with their diesels off and are quieter than a nuke and hard for us to detect. Supposedly they can swim circles around our giant nuclear subs."

"All true," Jason said. "After Blueback was decommissioned in 1990, the U.S. discontinued production of those smaller, quieter, conventionally powered, non-nuclear submarines. But because our nukes were too huge to use as diesel-electric stand-ins, we lost our ability to train in anti-submarine warfare against them. It wasn't long before our enemies figured out that all they had to do to defeat us was to buy surplus diesel-electric submarines and start using them."

"So, what did we do?" Aaron asked.

"We got smart and leased a diesel-electric from the Swedes. I personally trained alongside their crew for two years, learning everything there is to know about engaging them in anti-submarine warfare. I can assure you, U.S. nuclear submarines no longer have a problem detecting and killing diesel-electrics."

"Fascinating," Aaron said. "Sounds like you were doing great in the Navy, and being relatively young. Why'd you retire?"

Jason paused. "I didn't. I was dishonorably discharged."

"Whoa," Aaron said. "What'd you do to deserve *that?*"

Jason really didn't care to discuss that chapter of his career, and he thought an honest answer would end the discussion. "My brother needed my help, and when I asked for a day off, the Navy said no. So I went AWOL for the day."

"That must have been hard for you," Aaron said, trying to understand.

A look of bitter evil fell over Jason's face. "Believe me," he said. "It was."

Suddenly Aaron felt very uncomfortable. He glanced at his watch. "You know — I should be heading back. I have a long sail ahead of me." He stood up from the booth. "Thank you for the beer."

"But you haven't finished your burger," Brandy protested.

Aaron knew that, and it saddened him to leave it, but he really did have a long journey back. He held his hand over his stomach as if he'd eaten too much already. "I'm really full, thanks."

"Maybe we'll see you around the islands," Brandy said.

"Maybe so," Aaron said, and he and Jason shook hands.

As he turned to go, Brandy gave him a sexy little smile and a fluttering wave of her fingers. "Bye, Aaron," she said.

"What was *that* all about?" Jason said.

"What," Brandy said.

"You know very well, *what*. All that goo-goo-ga-ga over Aaron — *that's what*. I thought I was going to puke."

Brandy took a big sip of her beer and said, "I don't know what you're talking about."

Jason took an even bigger sip. He had plenty more to say, but he chose to hold his tongue. Brandy thought it best to do the same.

Lunch came and it was excellent, but it was eaten in silence.

Chapter 16

It was nearly dark when Aaron sailed up to the beach on the northern most Cayman Island called Cayman Brac. It had been a long return sail, and he was happy to be back at the place he called home. He rammed the keel of the boat up onto the sand and then hopped out and tied the bow line to a nearby palm tree.

A few yards up the slope, a small hut sat perched on a flat slab of rock. Aaron followed the sandy, seashell-strewn path to the door (something he never bothered to lock) and stepped inside.

Little more than a bamboo box equipped with a window, a kitchenette, and a small bathroom, Aaron's tiny house wasn't much to write home about; but ever since the accident he had learned to live like a pauper, and this miniature beachfront resort suited him just fine.

He tossed his keys on the counter, lit a candle, and then pulled a fifth of Jack Daniels out of his only cupboard. He smiled when he saw that it was a new bottle: there was something deeply satisfying in peeling off the wrapper and cracking the seal on a new bottle of Jack. He slid a paper cup off a stack and set it on the counter next to the whiskey, and then opened the tiny fridge and yanked the ice tray out of the frosted hole that served as his freezer. He tapped the tray on the edge of the counter to free the two remaining cubes then dropped the cubes into the cup before refilling the tray and returning it to the freezer.

He picked up an old copy of the *Cayman Islands Gazette*, noticing a reprint of an article from the early 1900s about a submariner who'd been "shot" out of a torpedo tube.

That would be a lousy way to die, he thought.

Suddenly, an idea for a simple short story popped into his head, and as a writer he knew he had to get it down on paper before it vanished into the aether. He reached for a small notepad and pencil, flipped open the pad, and wrote five brief lines of text with five words per line. Then he tore the page off, folded it carefully, and put it in his pocket.

That done, and with the bottle and cup in hand, Aaron walked over and sat down on the beat-up velvet sofa that also served as his bed. He opened the bottle and poured the whiskey over the ice cubes until they floated freely; then he put his feet up on his sagging, bamboo coffee table and took a big sip.

The alcohol burned pleasantly going down, and for a moment Aaron was at peace, staring out the window at the tranquil, moonlit Caribbean.

But then, as it did every evening, his subconscious released into his conscious mind a flood of painful memories. It had been over two years, now, yet the images of those fateful three days were still as vivid and powerful as if they had happened yesterday. He recalled the insanity of the bank robbery, and the agony of being shot, and how back in the fish cannery, after saving his life, Needles and Beeks had laid him on a sofa very similar to the one he was sitting on now. He recalled his wild morphine dream, and how, throughout the painful ordeal, his best friend, Willy, had remained at his side.

He and his mother had lived through hell those three days, and had been so very close to starting a new life, the life they had hoped to rebuild after that dreadful night, when Aaron was nine, and the notifying officer and medic made their midnight house call to tell his mother that his father had been killed in action.

Then, in the blink of an eye, a black Hummer stole everything he had, everything except the one thing he had wanted to lose — those painful memories.

He took another sip of whiskey and found himself pondering his earlier lunchtime encounter with the two yacht owners. He didn't know what to make of Brandy Fine's obvious, if not blatant, attraction to him, or the unsettling notion that he had met Jason Beckham before. But deep down he knew that, whether he liked it or not, he would be seeing the two of them again.

He took one last sip of whiskey, and then he lay back and closed his eyes, trusting that very soon the alcohol would carry him far away, giving him the courage to continue living a life that had lost all meaning.

THURSDAY

Chapter 17

"Permission to come aboard?"

Jason turned toward the sound of a familiar voice and smiled when he saw the man standing on the dock. "Permission granted!" he yelled back. The man came on board the *Cayman Jewel* and the two exchanged a hearty hand-shake.

"It's good to see you, my friend," Jason said. "What's it been, five years?"

"At least," the man replied.

Brandy was lounging up on the foredeck. She had spotted the stranger in the expensive suit as he passed through the marina gate. Jason called to her and she came down to join them on the main deck.

"Brandy, I'd like you to meet my dear friend, Commander Richard Fagan, of the United States Navy," Jason said. "Commander Fagan, meet Brandy Fine."

Fagan took her hand and kissed the back of it.

Wow, Brandy thought, blushing a little. *That's not something you see every day.*

"You're a lucky man, Jason," Fagan said, giving her hand a gentle squeeze before letting go.

His hand was strong and powerful, like Jason's. Brandy wished he'd been in uniform and was curious as to why he wasn't. She would have loved to stay and talk about it, but thought it best not interrupt a meeting between two naval officers. She excused herself and headed below decks.

Fagan looked around at the expanse of teak decking, polished white fiberglass, and brass accents sparking in the midmorning light. "You've done well for yourself, Jason," he said.

Jason felt a twinge of guilt and quickly changed the subject. What Fagan didn't know wouldn't hurt him. "You're the last man I would have expected to see this morning," he said. "Especially way down here in the Caymans. I'm surprised you found me." He really *was* surprised that Fagan had found him so easily. He had worked hard to keep a low profile, and Fagan's sudden appearance was a little unnerving.

"A tip from a young man at Earl's Reef Dive Shop, on Cayman Brac," Fagan admitted. "Nice kid. Very accommodating."

Jason kicked himself for giving Aaron Quinn the impression that he welcomed visitors.

"We should sit down," he said, gesturing toward a private yet spacious lounge area on the aft deck with an unobstructed view of the Caribbean Sea.

Fagan took the same seat the dead tourist was occupying when Jason shot him in the head. He sat forward and clasped his hands in front of him.

"I'm sure you've figured out that I'm not here by accident," he said, "so I'll get right to the point. I've recently become part of a small team of important men with big plans, and we're in the final planning stages of a mission of great importance."

"I'm listening ..." Jason said.

"I was asked if I knew anyone outside of the military who could pilot a submarine. And, well ... I thought of you."

Jason was taken aback. *Pilot a submarine? What on earth for?* It had been years since he'd been in the Navy, and he hadn't so much as *looked* at the controls of anything other than his old cabin-cruiser, and the *Cayman Jewel*, of course. Besides, his dishonorable discharge pretty much guaranteed he would *never* set foot on a sub again.

"Richard, I'm flattered," he said. "But I haven't —"

"Just listen for second," Fagan said. "I'd expect you to have lost most of your chops by now. But do you remember when the Swedes came over to Point Loma with their submarine, HMS Gotland?"

"Of course," Jason said. "They were here for two years. I spent so much time aboard that little diesel I could practically sail it all by myself."

"Well, the sub I'm talking about is nearly identical to the Gotland," Fagan said. "You should know her like the back of your hand."

Jason knew that what Fagan was saying was true. With a proper crew, and when compared with the massive nuclear submarines he had piloted toward the end of his career, sailing an old, Soviet, Cold-War era, diesel-electric attack sub would be a walk in the park.

"Where is this sub of yours? What's her name?" Jason asked.

"She was christened b-39," Fagan said. "She's moored down at the MMSD on San Diego Bay."

"I've read about that boat," Jason said. "Code named Cobra, formerly known as the 'terror of the deep'. One of the Soviet Project 641 submarines classified as "Foxtrot" by

NATO. Essentially larger and more powerful versions of German World War II era U-boats. Low-tech but lethal."

"I'm impressed," Fagan said.

"Yes, but you know better than I do, Richard, she hasn't left the museum's docks since she *got* there. She's nothing but a crumbling tourist attraction, covered with temporary stairs, walkways, and railings. Why on earth would you attempt to —"

"We think she has one more mission in her," Fagan said, interrupting Jason. They had a lot to discuss in a short amount of time. "But I'm not at liberty to tell you what that mission will be — not just yet."

Jason was curious, now. "How could we sail away from a busy Harbor Drive dock without being discovered? Tourists are everywhere." But no sooner had he said it did it dawn on him.

"It is common practice for shipyards to erect large, semi-permanent, plastic tarpaulins, or shelters, to protect ships from the elements while under construction or repair," Fagan said.

"And from prying eyes," Jason said. "We simply drive out from underneath the tarp running on battery power, right?"

"Right," Fagan said. "My connections at the Maritime Museum of San Diego and the San Diego Port Authority have spread the word that b-39 is in need of minor repair and will be under cover and closed to the public for thirty-six hours. No one will ever know she's gone."

"The water's only twenty feet deep in that part of the bay," Jason said. "We'd have to claw our way out."

"We'll be squashing stingrays for sure, but there's plenty of depth once we reach the main channel."

Jason knew that, of course, but it all seemed too surreal. He considered for a moment. It would help if he knew what they were proposing to do.

Fagan removed his suit jacket and laid it over a deck chair. He sensed Jason's trepidation and figured it was time to throw him something tangible.

"Listen," he said. "I know this all sounds a bit crazy. So I've arranged a meeting, this Sunday, in Coronado, and I'd like for you to attend. You'll get answers to all of your questions, first-hand, from b-39's former captain himself."

Jason's immediate reaction was negative and he spoke without thinking. "Why should I go all the way to San Diego to meet with some old sea-fart, when you can't give me the slightest hint as to what you're up to."

Jason's cavalier attitude and blatant disrespect for Captain Pankov offended Commander Fagan — he hadn't traveled more than half way around the world in the last two days to suffer the whining of a crybaby. But Jason was the right man for the job, and Fagan knew it.

"*Damn* you, Jason," he said, struggling to maintain his composure. "Do you think I would have traveled all the way down here to fucking Grand Cayman to speak with you in person if I didn't think it would be worth your while? What's the matter with you? Trust me for once, okay? You'll want to be in on this."

He removed an envelope from his inside breast pocket and handed it to Jason. "That's a first-class round-trip ticket to San Diego. We're meeting for brunch in the Crown Room at the Del at 11:00 a.m. Sunday. I'll have a car waiting for you outside San Diego International at 10:30. The driver will carry a sign reading BLACK COBRA."

Jason turned the plane ticket over in his hands, feeling a bit foolish. He couldn't respond with any clarity, so he didn't try.

Fagan glanced at his watch — he had done all he could. It was up to Jason now.

"I have a plane to catch," he said, rising to his feet. "I hope to see you Sunday. If you decide to show, I'll propose a toast in your honor."

Jason walked Fagan to the marina gate, and they shook hands goodbye.

Jason returned to the yacht and flopped down on a lounge chair overlooking the water. His head was spinning.

What was that all about? he thought, rubbing his temples. *Flying all the way up to San Diego for an out-of-the-blue mystery meeting with some old Russian submariner?* It was insane.

He took another look at the plane ticket and then slipped it into his pocket and closed his tired eyes.

Sunday
Three days later ...

San Diego

Chapter 18

Jason stepped out of the limousine in front of the Hotel Del Coronado shading his eyes from the Southern California sun.

His flight in from Grand Cayman had been delayed, and he'd been forced to sprint half-way across San Diego International to get to the waiting limo on time. Two years in the Caribbean had taken a bigger toll on his fitness than he had thought, and as he started up the red carpet runner he realized how tired he was.

Commander Fagan had rightly assumed that Jason would show up at the important meeting sorely underdressed, and on the ride over to Coronado, Jason found a designer suit, a silk shirt and tie, a slim leather belt, and a pair of hand-made Italian loafers with socks sealed in a garment bag next to him on the seat. It was clear that Fagan had gone to a lot of trouble, so Jason acquiesced, swapping his T-shirt and jeans for the suit.

Fagan had reserved a table overlooking the Pacific Ocean in the Del's fabulous Crown Room, a cavernous space, with 30-foot-high, hand-carved wooden ceilings, capable of seating over 600 diners.

Jason checked his watch, 10:59 a.m. It was a miracle he had made it there on time. He straightened his tie, buttoned his jacket, and entered the famous restaurant from the north side through the set of heavy, wooden double-doors.

Jason looked around and spotted Richard Fagan seated at a table with two others at the far end of the room. He padded across the expanse of Victorian-era carpeting and approached the table. The three men stood to greet him.

Fagan handled the introductions. "Captain Vtorak Borisovich Pankov," he said, "I'd like you to meet Jason Souther."

"How do you do, sir?" Jason said, shaking hands with a man more than twice his age. His impression of the captain changed in an instant. Pankov was no ordinary old fart.

"It is a pleasure to finally meet you, Commander," Pankov said, giving Jason's hand a vigorous Russian-style shake.

His accent was strong but his English excellent, and Jason did a double-take at being called *Commander* again. "Thank you, sir, but I prefer Jason," he said.

From what Richard Fagan had told him, Pankov had expected Jason to be a little more rough around the edges. "The suit looks good, Jason," he said.

"Yes, sir," Jason said, a tad embarrassed. He would thank Richard later.

Pankov turned to the fourth man at the table, a man about five years his junior. "This is my friend and loyal confidant, Captain Uri Ruden," he said. "Himself a distinguished former Soviet submariner."

Uri was pleased to hear that Pankov's memory was sharper today. He shook Jason's hand across the table. "How do you do, Jason?" he said. "My thanks to Commander Fagan for finding you."

"Thank you," Jason said, accepting the compliment. "I thought it couldn't be done."

Pankov found that amusing. He smiled and looked at Fagan. "For a man of Richard's caliber it was an easy task — like pulling candy from a baby."

Jason smiled at Pankov's inaccurate attempt at the American idiom.

"Please have a seat," Fagan said, gesturing to an empty chair, and they all sat down at the table.

Pankov had Jason's leather-bound dossier in front of him. He turned to a marked page. "There is one thing puzzling me, Jason," he said, more serious now. "It is about your dishonorable discharge. Why would you go AWOL from the United States Navy simply to visit your brother in prison for a day, knowing full well it may ruin your career as an officer? Is that not a bit extreme?"

Jason looked at him and for a moment considered walking out. Instead he took a deep breath and gathered himself.

"My mother and father died in a private plane crash when I was two," he explained. "My big brother, my only sibling, was only nineteen at the time, and for ten years he set aside his dreams and aspirations to raise me. I tried to repay him for everything he'd done for me, of course, but I failed miserably, and he continued to bail me out whenever I was in trouble."

He took a sip of water.

"Finally he took the rap for an armed, bank robbery that was all my idea and, while I walked, he picked up twenty. Johnny was one tough son-of-a-bitch, and he could hold his own in any fight, but at San Quentin things were different.

He was just one man against many. I thought if I could just talk to him, and maybe help him out somehow, it might offset the huge debt I owed him. Don't you see? I at least had to try."

"Was it worth it?" Uri asked.

"Yes, Uri, it was," Jason said. "My presence in San Quentin that day gave Johnny a renewed self-confidence, and inmates who had paid no attention to him in the past took a liking to him and started fighting alongside him. He went from having a life expectancy approaching zero to having his own army. I'd do it again in a second."

"Why did you not tell me this?" Fagan said.

"It was my problem ... not yours," Jason said.

Satisfied with Jason's answer, Pankov continued. "What we will ask you to do this morning will make you a rich man, Jason."

Jason's heart slid up into his throat.

"However, make no mistake," Pankov added, "you will earn every penny."

That sent Jason's mind swimming. He hadn't the slightest idea what was coming next, but he already knew his answer would be yes.

"If you choose to join us in this endeavor," Pankov said, "several things will be set into motion immediately." He sat up in his chair and picked up a menu. "But first we must eat. Commander Fagan tells me the food here is excellent."

Chapter 19

The four officers dined on a tempting variety of prepared-to-order omelets, benedicts, and other breakfast classics, supported by gourmet cheeses, charcuterie, sushi, king crab, lobster bisque, and hand-carved prime rib. Dessert choices included a chocolate fountain, a truffle tower, tiramisu, caramel flan, cobblers, tarts, cakes, and more.

Brunch included freshly squeezed mimosas and screwdrivers, and Pankov reminisced about the daily ration of white wine served to the crew aboard b-39 — a ration they commonly refused as not being the much preferred and officially banned vodka.

Fagan pointed out that the exquisitely detailed chandeliers there in the Crown Room were designed by none other than the author of *The Wonderful Wizard of Oz*, L. Frank Baum. Jason mentioned that Charles Lindbergh celebrated his famous transatlantic flight there, as well.

Pankov and Uri Ruden had heard of Lindbergh, of course, and both had seen the film adaptation of Baum's book, so they were duly impressed.

Over coffee, Jason felt comfortable enough to broach the subject of his hiring. "Captain Pankov," he said. "You were saying that if I take the job, several things would be set into motion immediately."

"That is correct," Pankov said, wiping his chin with a cloth napkin. "First and foremost, an account, in a sympathetic Grand Cayman bank, will be set up in your name with a balance of $5 million. Half held in trust, half available to you immediately." He paused for effect.

Jason sucked in a quick breath and gripped his knees under the table.

"The job will take place in roughly one month, here in San Diego," Pankov said. "I thought perhaps if you and your girlfriend wanted to cruise up here on your yacht, you should have enough time to do so, and in order to help facilitate that, and as a second incentive, I will see to it that your beloved *Cayman Jewel* is properly registered, here in the U.S., in your name, with all historical paperwork and necessary licenses."

Jason shot a sheepish glance Fagan's way: Why he'd thought he could fool someone with his high level of intelligence, he didn't know.

"Finally," Pankov said, "as a third incentive, we will have your dishonorable discharge from the U.S. Navy expunged from your record, and in its place, the *honorable* military discharge you deserve." He took a sip of his coffee, allowing his words to sink in.

Jason's eyes moistened and he wanted to cry out with joy. Fagan had obviously played a big role in the selection of incentives.

Stay calm, he thought. *You still don't know what you must do in exchange.* He took a sip of coffee and kept his mouth shut.

"We're looking for someone capable of handling *any and all* submarine operations," Commander Fagan said, "because that is what will be demanded of each of us. To say we'll be running a skeleton crew would be a gross understatement, and I thought of you because I know you can handle it."

"How many crewmen are we talking about?" Jason asked.

"Including you, we'll have four," Fagan said.

"*Four?*" Jason said. "Are you serious?" He looked at the others and considered for a moment. "The four at this table, I presume?"

"That's right," Fagan said.

Jason paused for a moment. "Who outside this group knows about your plan?"

"Only one other," Fagan said. "A man whom you'll meet at a later date."

Pankov cleared his throat and looked squarely into Jason's eyes. "Our mission is classified as top-secret, Jason, and must be treated as such, or there will be *deadly* consequences. Do you understand this?"

"Y-yes, of course, Captain," Jason said.

"What Commander Fagan hasn't told you," Pankov went on, "and what I'm prepared to tell you now, is that we are planning an assassination ... a *political assassination.*"

Jason concealed a look of shock. This really *was* serious. "May I ask who it is that we'll be assassinating?" he ventured.

Captain Pankov glanced at his colleagues, then closed Jason's dossier and looked at him. "Suffice it to say, the target is a high-ranking official in the United States government."

"But why the sub?"

"We're going to take this guy out the old fashion way," Pankov said. "With a torpedo."

GRAND CAYMAN

Chapter 20

It was dark when Brandy spotted Jason walking through the marina security gate. She had had time to think about things, and although he had only been gone for the day, she had missed him. She hopped up and skipped down the gangway to greet him.

"Welcome home, sweetie!" she cried, giving him a flying hug that nearly put both of them in the water.

"Whoa, there," Jason said, regaining his balance. "I take it you're glad to see me." He dropped his bag on the deck and gave her a big kiss. "I was gone less than a day, you know."

"I know, but it felt like years," she said. "I want to hear all about your trip."

The two boarded the *Cayman Jewel* and Brandy made drinks while Jason got settled.

It was a warm evening, and the air smelled sweet. Brandy snuggled up with Jason on a lounge chair.

"So ... how did it go?" she asked.

"It went well," Jason replied, taking a sip of his drink. The full scope of the meeting hadn't really sunk in yet and he had trouble coming up with a way to explain it. "Brunch was fantastic. Just as I remembered it."

"What was the meeting about? What did they say?"

He wanted to tell her about the money, but after promising her diamonds, he figured he'd better wait until he'd been to the bank. "Not much really," he said. "They want me to pilot a submarine for them."

"What? Really? That's *crazy*."

"I know."

"But where? Why?"

"In San Diego. I have to report there in a few weeks."

"For how long?"

"For a while, I guess, but don't worry, you're coming too. In fact we'll both be moving there."

Brandy's mind whirled with a mix of emotions. She was relieved that Jason wasn't leaving without her, but leaving her home in the Caymans for who knows what in San Diego? "But what about the *Cayman Jewel*? She is our home."

"The *Jewel* will still be our home. We're going to sail her up there."

Brandy paused. "Do you think we could do that? Just the two of us? San Diego's a long way from here."

"I know that," Jason said. "I'm thinking about asking Aaron to come along, just to be sure."

A thrill ran up Brandy's spine. "Aaron Quinn? Would he do that?"

Jason took another sip. "I'm not sure. But it can't hurt to ask."

Monday

Chapter 21

The lobby in Cayman Union Bank reminded Jason of the bank he and Johnny were robbing when they got caught. He looked around nervously for a minute and then approached the counter.

"May I help you?" the cashier said. She was pretty and polite. His new banking relationship was off to a good start.

"Uh — yes," he said. "There's an account in the name of Jason Souther. I'd like a printout of the balances, please."

"May I see some form of ID?"

Jason provided the ID and the cashier printed out the report.

"Will there be anything else?" she said, checking to see that he wasn't wearing a wedding ring.

"This will be fine," he said, and took the report outside.

He found a bench in the shade and sat down to look over the report. His eyes went wide. The total account balance including trusts was $5 million. Available balance: $2.5 million. The money was his. Pankov was for *real*.

Jason folded the statement and put it in his pocket. Then he went back inside and made a cash withdrawal in the amount of $2,500.

Chapter 22

Aaron was up at Earl's Reef Dive Shop busily refilling SCUBA tanks when Jason showed up.

"I didn't expect to see *you* here," Aaron said, surprised.

"Good to see you, Aaron," Jason said. "Do you have a minute?"

"Yeah — uh, sure ..." He indicated a picnic table down by the water. "Have a seat down at that table. I'll be right there."

Aaron killed the air compressor and secured the refilled tanks, and then joined Jason.

"What's up?" Aaron said, folding his hands in front of him.

Jason decided to get right to the point. "Brandy and I are going to sail the *Cayman Jewel* up to San Diego ... and, well, we could use an extra hand. I thought maybe you'd like to come along."

That was the last thing Aaron had expected. "That's a long trip," he said, picturing the route from the Cayman Islands to San Diego on an imaginary map. "Why would you want to do *that*?"

"I have work there, consulting on some kind of restoration project."

"But I have a job here," Aaron said.

"I know," Jason said. "But I thought if you could get a leave of absence, your job will be waiting for you when you get back. I'll fly you straight back to the Caymans once we arrive in San Diego."

This all sounded a bit crazy to Aaron. He really didn't know how to respond. "How long do you figure the trip will take?" he asked.

"The *Cayman Jewel*'s cruise speed is eighteen knots," Jason said, "with a top speed of twenty three knots. So in terms of international travel, we're not that fast. I've never made the run myself, but I'm figuring two weeks, maybe three. There's a welcome party in San Diego in twenty days that I really want to attend."

Aaron recalled his original trip to the Cayman's with the retired couple. It had been quite an experience, but he wasn't sure he was ready to do it *again*. "I'd like to think about it," he said.

"Of course," Jason said. "But we leave Friday."

"*This* Friday?" Aaron said.

"I'll have you meet me at the marina Thursday afternoon," Jason said. "To help with the final preparations."

"That's not much time," Aaron said. "Can I let you know?"

"I'll know you're interested when you show up," Jason said.

He stood up to leave, giving Aaron a thumbs up. "*Carpe diem*, Aaron," he said.

Thursday

Chapter 23

Thursday afternoon, as scheduled, Aaron showed up at the marina with his duffle bag. He had been granted a leave of absence by the manager at Earl's Reef Dive Shop and had every intention of returning to his job on Cayman Brac immediately after the trip.

He helped Jason load the last of the provisions on board the *Cayman Jewel,* then they walked up to the marina office to square up with the manager.

The marina manager was a native islander with a heavy accent. "Good afternoon, Mr. Jason," he said. "I am sad to hear you are leaving us for a while." He had some papers ready and slid them forward.

"Just for a few weeks," Jason said. "If I can I'd like to keep my same slip."

"No problem ..." the manager said, checking the marina rules in his head. "We'll hold the electric, water, and phone for you, but the slip rental accrues, of course."

"Of course," Jason said, and he began filling out the paperwork.

"Two men were just here looking for you," the manager said.

Jason looked up, surprised. He'd been dreading hearing those words again, words he hadn't heard in a long time.

"Just now? he said. "What did they want? You didn't tell them anything ..."

"No, sir, Mr. Jason," the manager said. "I would never do that. You are my friend."

Brandy sat alone on deck enjoying a nice garden salad. In honor of another beautiful day in paradise, she wore nothing but a thong bikini with a *very* skimpy top.

"Ahoy there," a man's voice called from the dock.

Brandy looked over the railing and saw two men in Hawaiian shirts approaching the *Cayman Jewel*.

"*Coming,*" she called. She wiped her hands on a towel and headed over to the gangway to investigate.

"Pardon the intrusion, miss," the shorter man said. "I was hoping you could answer a couple of questions."

Brandy could spot a shoulder holster a mile away — even under a baggy floral pattern.

"You guys cops?" she said, glancing up toward the marina office. She wondered why Jason hadn't seen them first.

"I guess you would consider this a social visit," the man said. "I'm James Harness, and this is my good friend Larry Holt." Harness had thought of using fake names, but he knew this lead was a long shot anyway, so he didn't bother.

"Pleased to meet you, ma'am," Holt said, nodding politely.

Brandy looked up at him. She had never seen a black man both that huge and that good looking. *You should take up acting,* she thought.

"I'm Brandy," she said, shaking their hands.

The men struggled to maintain their composure. Standing that close to a half-naked woman as stunning and fragrant as

Brandy without dropping their pants was proving difficult, if not impossible.

Brandy sensed this, of course, and it sent a thrill up her leg.

"I was wondering if you knew this man," Harness said at last. He handed her a photo that Holt had dug up somewhere. "He and I met back in the States a couple of years ago, and since I'm rarely in the area, I thought I'd look him up."

Brandy took a look at the picture and smiled to herself: she had never seen Jason in his Naval Officer's dress uniform — and he looked *amazing*.

"Never seen him before," she said calmly, wondering how this stranger found out where Jason lived.

Harness searched Brandy's eyes. She was hiding something — he was sure of it. He took out a pad and pen and jotted down his number.

"Sorry to have disturbed you, miss," he said. "If you happen to see him would you give me a call? It would be great to talk to him again."

"I could do that," Brandy said.

"We appreciate your time," Harness said.

He started to leave, but as a detective he couldn't resist giving Brandy a little something extra to think about. "Keep an eye out, will you?" he said. "One of the locals thought maybe Jason lived right here in this marina."

He gave her a nod that said, *Chew on that for a while, bitch,* and then he and Holt started back down the gangway.

Just then Jason and Aaron came out of the marina office. Jason stopped when he spotted the two men coming up the ramp. He thought he recognized the shorter one from somewhere, but the Hawaiian shirt threw him, and he figured he must be mistaken.

"*What's going on?*" Aaron whispered, trying to follow Jason's gaze.

Suddenly Jason stepped back a step and took hold of Aaron's arm. There was no mistake: It was *him* ... the cop that shot him in the leg that night in Sally's Diner!

"Come with me," he said, and they ducked behind a portable restroom.

Harness and Holt continued up the ramp and entered the marina office.

The marina manager looked at Harness expectantly.

"He wasn't there," Harness said. "Only some woman named Brandy."

"He must have stepped out," the manager said.

Harness laid a crisp $50 on the counter. "If you see him, there's more where that came from," he said.

He made a mental note to return to the *Cayman Jewel* later that evening, and then he and Holt turned to leave.

"Why did you *pay* him again?" Holt said as they entered the parking lot. "You know as well as I do he's a lying sack of shit."

Harness unlocked their rented Mustang, ignoring Holt. He knew the man was lying, of course, but he also knew that maintaining a healthy dialogue was worth a little cash.

Jason and Aaron watched the men drive away, and then they returned to the *Cayman Jewel.*

Brandy was just finishing her salad. She stood up when Jason and Aaron came on board, anxious to tell Jason about her two visitors.

"We sail tonight," Jason said gruffly, walking straight past her. He headed downstairs to the galley.

"Why tonight?" Brandy asked Aaron, but Aaron only shrugged.

They followed Jason below.

Jason opened the fridge and then slammed it closed in frustration. "Isn't there any food on this tub?" he said. It was a ridiculous question, of course, considering they had just stocked the boat for a long trip.

"There were two men here, Jason," Brandy insisted. "They were asking about you. They had a picture of you and they were packing heat."

"Was one in his mid-fifties?" Jason asked sarcastically. "The other a handsome black man around six-five? Both dressed like tourists?"

"You *saw them?*" Brandy said, feeling foolish. "Why didn't you say something?"

Jason opened the fridge again, grabbed a beer, and slammed the door. Then he went back up on deck.

Brandy looked at Aaron, but again he only shrugged.

Chapter 24

Sailing just before nightfall, Jason found the going easy. It felt good to be out on the open water again, a warm breeze in his face, away from whoever might be looking for him. Sailing was the only thing that brought peace to his soul.

He switched the *Cayman Jewel* to auto pilot and joined Aaron and Brandy on the aft deck.

"We should make good time tonight," he said. "There's no wind to speak of and the sea is as flat as a billiard table."

Aaron had mapped out the trip to San Diego in his head. "I assume we're taking the Panama Canal route," he said. "Do they even *allow* private yachts through there, with all of the huge cargo ships and cruise ships going in and out?"

"I can't say it will be easy," Jason admitted. "We'll be like a skateboard on a freeway. But private yachtsmen do it every day. We'll hire an agent to help us with the paperwork and navigation, and we'll be measured and fees calculated based on our theoretical cargo capacity. As we approach the Canal Zone we'll be in contact with traffic control at Flemenco, keeping them informed regarding our location and speed. It's a one to three day trip through the canal, depending upon how good our agent is at schmoozing the authorities."

"The authorities can cause problems for us?" Aaron asked.

"I'm not too concerned," Jason said. "Canal agents have a reputation for getting things done."

Brandy was shocked. She had figured that crossing the Panama Canal would take about an hour.

"I'm especially looking forward to crossing Lake Gatun," Jason said. "It makes up a large portion of the canal, and I should be able to relax for a while with no locks to worry about. Overall it should be a very interesting crossing."

"How long will the whole trip take?" Brandy asked.

"Two to three weeks," Jason said. "I'm figuring four or five days from the Caymans to Panama, another one to three days on the canal, maybe five days up to Cabo, followed by two or three days sailing to San Diego."

"Do we have to worry about 'The Pirates of the Caribbean'?" Aaron asked, only half kidding.

Brandy looked at him, surprised. That possibility had never occurred to her.

Jason smiled. "I'd be lying if I said we didn't. But according to the International Maritime Bureau's Piracy Reporting Centre, the two countries to be concerned about in this region are Brazil and Peru. We're sailing to Panama by way of Honduras, Nicaragua, and Costa Rica, hugging the coastline, and Central America is not on the bureau's current list."

Brandy sat back in her seat, dazed. This adventure was turning out to be a lot more than she had bargained for.

Chapter 25

Jason Souther had done an excellent job covering his tracks over the last two years, and for Harness and Holt, sniffing themselves all the way from their tiny East Coast precinct office to Grand Cayman in the Cayman Islands had taken a considerable amount of skill, more than a little luck, and most of their strength and stamina; and although they had come up empty at the marina the first time around, the intrepid duo were confident that, at long last, they were hot on Jason's trail.

After grabbing a quick bite to eat, they decided to stop by the Cayman Union Bank, figuring that if Jason *were* living on Grand Cayman he would likely have an account there. But it was no use. The island's legendary banking system was every bit as secretive as they'd heard it would be.

With their confidence still high, the men dropped back by the marina to pay another visit to the *Cayman Jewel*.

But her slip was empty.

They scanned the rest of the marina, figuring they'd somehow been confused as to the yacht's actual location, but to no avail.

They went to the marina office and questioned the manager, and he confirmed that the yacht was indeed gone — out to sea for an indeterminate amount of time, destination unknown.

Harness had lost Jason Souther *again*.

Tired and frustrated, Harness sat on a bench, trying to come to grips with the fact that he had failed, and that Jason's trail and most of Holt's savings had dried up.

He and his loyal partner would have no choice but to fly home to the States with their tails between their legs and try their best to mend their broken careers.

But before they did, Harness wanted to make one more stop.

Chapter 26

Two years had passed since Harness helped save a young boy's life back at Sally's Diner, and since then, hardly a day had gone by when he hadn't thought of him.

He had heard that after being released from the hospital, the boy had left the country, leaving a trail when he applied for a work visa in the Cayman Islands. Harness knew that this, too, was an extreme long shot, but after questioning a few Cayman locals he was told that there was a young man that fit the description living up on Cayman Brac, working at a dive shop called Earl's Reef.

He and Holt drove straight to the airport and boarded the next plane to Cayman Brac, betting on a chance to say hello to Aaron Quinn.

"You just missed him," the salty man behind the counter at Earl's Reef Dive Shop told them. "Won't be back for a month ... that is if he ever *does* come back. Said something about sailing a motor-yacht through the Panama Canal, and in my experience, those folks, the ones that sail that far, never return. He'll be sorely missed around here."

Harness couldn't believe his luck. They had actually tracked Aaron down. It was a shame that they had missed him.

"Did he say where they were headed?" he asked, figuring he might run into Aaron sometime in the future.

"I can't recall," the man said. "But he did mention a flaming redhead who has the hots for him." He paused, scratching his whiskers. "There was something else ... Oh, yeah, I'm pretty sure he said the boat's captain was some guy named ... Jason."

Harness looked at Holt, unable to believe what he'd just heard. Holt couldn't believe it either.

"Did he mention the captain's last name?" Harness asked the man. "Or the name of the yacht?"

"Nope, only Jason."

Harness had to take a moment. There was no way that the guy Aaron was sailing with was Jason *Souther* ... or that the motor-yacht he and Aaron were on was the *Cayman Jewel*. That would be *way* too strange a coincidence. An impossible turn of fate.

He jotted down his number on a scrap of paper and handed it to the man. "If by some chance Aaron should happen to return, would you tell him I stopped by?"

"Yep," the man said. He dropped the note into a jar full of business cards.

Harness thanked the man, and then he and Holt left Earl's Reef and boarded a plane bound for Panama City.

FRIDAY
VLADIVOSTOK, RUSSIA

Chapter 27

Ekatarina Vtorakevna Pankova lived with her father in their modest home overlooking Vladivostok Harbor, along Russia's northern coast. She was in her bedroom, seated lightly on a small chair, smiling at her reflection in the vanity mirror, brushing her long black hair with enthusiasm.

She was going to see her boyfriend tonight. They had been dating for two years now, and she had a strong feeling that tonight would be the night he would ask for her hand in marriage.

She set the brush aside and lifted her breasts a little before letting them bounce, thinking, *Thank you my twin friends. You've served me well.*

There was a knock on her door, which she answered after quickly donning her robe.

"Yes, Father?" she said.

"There is something I need to discuss with you," Vtorak Pankov said.

Ekatarina glanced at the clock on her bedside table. "But I was just getting ready to go see Boris."

"Please, sit down," Pankov insisted.

Ekatarina hesitated and then took a seat on the edge of the bed.

Pankov pulled up a chair. "Ekatarina, my dear," he said. "Now that you are out of high school, you need to see the world."

She looked at her father. *I know that,* she thought. She was hoping to be married soon, and seeing the world was her plan.

"You and I are going to America for a while," Pankov said.

"*What?*" Ekatarina cried, incredulous. "Where?"

"California," he said. "San Diego to be precise."

"You can't be serious."

"We leave in three weeks."

Ekatarina couldn't believe what she was hearing. "You're just doing this because you don't like Boris!" she cried. "You know we plan to marry soon, and now you want to break us apart!"

"When my business there is finished we will return," Pankov said. "If Boris loves you as much as you think he does, he will wait for you."

Ekatarina grabbed her hair as if to tear it out in frustration. "How long?" she asked quickly. "How long will we be in America?"

Pankov knew he would not be coming back. But as for his daughter, it depended, of course, upon how the U.S. responded to the assassination.

"A few days, maybe a few weeks," he said. "If things go as planned."

"You're lying," Ekatarina said. "No one from Russia ever just *visits* the United States. You plan to *immigrate* and *keep me there forever!*" She rolled over onto the bed and buried her face in her pillow, sobbing.

"I don't expect you to understand," Pankov said calmly. "But this matter is of the utmost importance to our country. Some day you will realize that, and perhaps then you will forgive me. I will give you an exact departure date when I have one."

Then he went out.

TUESDAY
FOUR DAYS LATER ...

10 MILES OFF THE COAST OF COSTA RICA

Chapter 28

For Jason and his crew, the first few days of the voyage had run like fine clockwork. Refueling and resupply were easy, and the towns, restaurants, and bars they visited along the way were fantastic. Even Brandy had begun to relax, thinking maybe the trip wasn't going to be so bad after all.

At around 4:00 a.m., Tuesday, just before sunrise, 10 miles off the coast of Costa Rica, Aaron awoke to a strange, low buzz coming from somewhere on the water. He grabbed a pair of high-powered binoculars out of a cabinet and went to the window.

In the predawn light he could just make out what appeared to be four men in a small outboard approaching the *Cayman Jewel* at high speed, and as they drew nearer it was clear that they were carrying rifles. Jason had told Aaron what to watch out for, and there was little doubt that he was about to encounter his first pirates.

He jumped into some clothes and ran to the master cabin to alert Jason.

"How far out?" Jason said, pulling on his pants.

"About a mile," Aaron said.

"Go to the midships cabin and get my sniper rifle. There's an assault rifle as well … in the large drawer under the bed. Hurry!"

Aaron ran to the cabin and retrieved the rifles, along with a box of ammo for each.

He returned with the guns, and Jason took the AWSM. Aaron slid a magazine into the well of the assault rifle and clicked it home. Then he slapped it hard and gave it a tug to make sure it was seated.

"Looks like you know how to handle a rifle," Jason said, surprised.

"Actually, I do," Aaron said.

Jason finished assembling his rifle, listening for the approaching boat. "Time to rock, my friend," he said.

From up on deck they could clearly see the four men speeding toward them in their small outboard, and Aaron had been correct: they had guns.

"They're the real thing, all right," Jason said. "Friendlies would have signaled their intentions by now. These guys would as soon slit your throat as look at you."

Sweat moistened Aaron's palms.

The two positioned themselves and readied their rifles.

"I'll take out the one on the tiller," Jason said. "Hopefully that will discourage them. If they keep coming, I may need your help."

Aaron had sworn to himself that as long as he lived he would never touch a rifle in anger again. "Do we really have to shoot them?" he asked.

Suddenly they saw muzzle flashes and several bullets zinged by followed by the sound of gunfire.

"Holy *shit*," Aaron said, ducking. "I guess that answers my question." *Better them than us*, he thought miserably.

Jason put his eye to the scope and tracked his target. The boat bounded on the water making it a difficult shot. He controlled his breathing and slowly squeezed the trigger.

POP!

The man flipped backward over the outboard and the boat veered hard left. One of the remaining three quickly took the tiller, but instead of turning about and running, he cranked the throttle and keep right on coming. The other two men continued to fire off round after round.

Jason saw no choice but to waste all three of them, and he knew that if he hit the driver last this time, the boat would stay on course a fraction longer, giving both of them easier shots.

"You take the two on the right," he said. "I'll be right behind you."

Aaron held his breath, adrenaline coursing through his veins. The little boat seemed huge now, as muzzles flashed and bullets zipped by, tearing into the fiberglass and teak trim mere inches from his and Jason's heads.

"Steady," Jason said, taking aim again. "Smoke 'em if you got 'em."

Aaron sighted in on his targets, and through the scope he could see that the man nearest him had a large tattoo covering most of his face. He breathed deeply and between heartbeats squeezed the trigger.

POPOPOPOP!

The two men on the right side of the boat cartwheeled into the water just as Jason put a bullet between the eyes of their friend. The empty boat's motor stalled and it drifted to a stop, leaving nothing but an eerie silence.

"Well done," Jason said, raising a high-five.

Aaron was in shock, and hardly in the mood to celebrate, but he managed to five Jason back. "Oh my God," he said, still buzzing with adrenaline. "I thought they'd never quit!"

He ran his hand through his long hair, and then touched his finger to one of several bullet holes within easy reach.

"Just another night in the Caribbean," Jason said.

"Uh — yeah," Aaron said, wiping the sweat from his brow. He looked out across the water to make sure the pirates were truly gone. "Will there be more?"

"Most likely," Jason said. "But we're ready for them, right?" He patted the stock of his rifle.

"Right ..." Aaron said, feigning confidence. *Maybe this trip wasn't such a good idea after all*, he thought.

He found it a little unnerving that Jason was so comfortable using his sniper rifle to kill human beings, and suddenly he couldn't wait till they made it to San Diego.

"I should have hired you on years ago," Jason said. "You really know how to handle a rifle."

Aaron paused, looking down at his weapon. "I saved my mother's life with a gun very similar to this," he said sadly.

"Is that a fact," Jason said.

"Two years ago, back in the States."

"Where's your mother now?"

"She was killed in a hit-and-run. I almost died myself, but I was thrown clear before the car exploded. All I really remember is lying on a gurney talking to a detective before going to the hospital."

Jason suddenly felt a little uneasy, but he didn't know why. "Put the rifles back where you found them, will you? I'm going back to bed."

Aaron nodded and Jason went below.

Aaron took out the tattered business card he carried in his pocket. The faded lettering read:

DETECTIVE JAMES HARNESS

3rd Precinct

Brandy was in bed, clutching her blanket tightly under her chin.

Jason sat next to her. She'd been crying.

"All I could hear was that damn outboard motor coming closer and closer," she said. "Then the shots. I thought for sure we'd all be killed."

"It's over now," Jason said. "We'll be in San Diego before you know it."

She looked into his eyes. "I don't like sailing anymore," she said. "Let's turn around and go back to Grand Cayman. We're safer there. We're at *home* there. I just want to make love and eat cheeseburgers and drink beer."

Jason leaned over and gave her a hug and a lingering kiss. "Brandy," he said softly. "If you knew me at all, you'd know that's not going to happen."

Aaron gathered up the rifles and started for the stairs leading down to the midships cabin.

Suddenly something fearfully grotesque, brutally heavy, and soaking wet leaped on his back, sending him crashing to the deck. The side of his face hit the teak planking hard, nearly knocking him unconscious. The rifles clattered some distance away.

Dazed, and spitting blood, Aaron fought back blindly, but like a wild beast protecting its young, the man was viscous and powerful, and he quickly had Aaron in a hold that would surely break his neck. Aaron struggled desperately, his breath long since gone. Blue faced, eyes bulging, he managed to free one arm and retrieve his survival knife, and with no conscious thought he flipped it open and struck madly at his attacker's leg, driving the blade to the bone. The man cried out in pain, losing his hold on Aaron's neck. Aaron gasped for air and yanked his knife free, and then with everything he had he turned and drove it hard into his attacker's abdomen. Blood gushed over the knife as the man's shoulders jerked forward and his jaw opened wide; then his full weight fell upon Aaron, pinning him to the deck. With a last great effort, Aaron squeezed out from under him, freeing his knife. He crawled a few feet away, where he lay panting on the deck, exhausted, soaked to the skin with sweat, seawater, and blood. And then he passed out.

When Aaron came to, he felt like he'd been trod upon by an angry bull elephant. He felt sick, rolling over on his side to retch.

He glanced at the body lying nearby and was shocked to see that it was the pirate with the tattoo. It was patterned after a tropical flower, and covered the man's face, giving him a strange, hybrid appearance. The man's eyes were closed, but he wore the surprised, open mouthed look of a man unprepared to die.

In addition to the knife wounds, the man was bleeding profusely from an apparent bullet wound to his shoulder. Aaron's aim with the rifle had been good, but not good enough to kill.

How could he have fought so ferociously with an open gunshot wound? How could he swim that far?

He saw an empty sheath tied around the man's waist with a leather thong, and knew he had dodged a big one. The man's knife had no doubt gone to the bottom when he went swimming.

To his horror, Aaron thought he saw the man's chest slowly heave. He looked again. *Oh, my dear God*, he thought. *The ugly son-of-a-bitch isn't dead.*

Panic swelled in Aaron's heart. He had witnessed death before, but it had always been quick, and final — never an interminable lingering between life and death. He grasped the sticky handle of his survival knife tightly — ready to spring upon the man if he so much as flinched; but then he heard a low gurgling deep in the man's chest, and he knew that wouldn't be happening.

But the man wouldn't *die*.

I could stab him again, Aaron thought desperately. *Through the heart this time. O-or I could shoot him in the head. Certainly that would put an end to his misery.*

He glanced over at the assault rifle, but he couldn't bring himself to do it.

So he waited ... hearing nothing but the gurgle of the man's breathing, and the heavy, unsteady rhythm of his own beating heart.

Time slowed and the rising sun grew hotter. Aaron continued to look on in dazed confusion as the man's chest slowly rose and fell. His eyelids became too heavy to open, and he slipped back into unconsciousness.

When Aaron came to again, he tried not to look, but he knew the man with the tattoo would still be there.

The gurgling had stopped, and the man lay motionless.

Maybe he's finally dead, Aaron told himself. *Maybe it's just a body now.*

Suddenly the eyes opened, and in them such an extreme look of fright, that although the body remained still, for a moment Aaron thought all remaining life energy had gathered in them in a desperate attempt to flee the confines of the flesh, and rise up to the heavens, escaping the dreadful terror of an earthly death.

Aaron shuddered, wanting desperately to run away, but he couldn't move, nailed to the decking by the horror in a dying man's eyes.

And still the man *lived*.

Just then Jason Beckham came up from below decks. He took one look at Aaron, and the pirate, and then picked up the assault rifle and put a bullet through the man's tattooed forehead.

"Fucking hell, are you all right?" he said, kneeling next to Aaron. "Where the fuck did *he* come from?"

Aaron just lay there staring at the dead man. *You were trying to kill me, right? What else could I could do? What else could I possibly do?*

"Here, let's get you hosed off and back to bed," Jason said. "You look like you've gone fifteen with the devil himself." He helped Aaron to his feet and then showed him downstairs to his cabin.

WEDNESDAY
THE PANAMA CANAL

Chapter 29

PHOOOOOOOOOOT!

Aaron awoke in his cabin to the sound of a ship's horn. He checked his phone. 9:00 a.m. *Wednesday*. He had slept for 26 hours.

He leaned over and drew back the curtain and looked out the window. All he could see was a wall of white steel. A cruise ship was passing them on their starboard side. The ship's name was *Neau Islander*.

At first Aaron thought Jason had foundered into a shipping lane, a dangerous thing to do with a boat the size of the *Cayman Jewel*. But another look revealed the truth: after cruising 600 or 700 miles due south, they had, at long last, made it to the Panama Canal.

From his cabin window the locks looked huge. Aaron felt like an ant riding a leaf down a storm drain.

He rose and showered, and as he pulled on his jeans he heard a knock on his cabin door. He quickly added a T-shirt, then answered the door.

It was Brandy.

"I heard the shower," she said. "I thought you'd *never* wake up. Would you care for a little company?"

Aaron wasn't sure what she meant by that. "I'm not sure that's a good idea," he said. "Jason may need our help."

"Oh, relax. He'll be busy navigating the Gatun locks for hours. If he needs anything, his canal agent is with him."

"But what if he catches us? Here in my room, I mean. That would *not* be good."

"He won't," Brandy said, stepping into Aaron's cabin. "He told me not to disturb him until we reach Lake Gatun. He won't be expecting me until then. Besides, we're just talking, right?"

She looked at Aaron with her head turned slightly to the side. Then, to Aaron's surprise, she closed the cabin door and slowly unzipped a little purse, dumping the contents on the bed: a cut-off drinking straw, a razor blade, a small mirror, and a gram of cocaine.

A foil-wrapped condom fell out as well. "Oops," Brandy said, smiling coyly as she returned it to the purse. "I don't think we'll be needing *that*."

Aaron watched wide-eyed as Brandy unfolded the packet of coke and poured a small portion of the powder onto the mirror, and then she used the blade to chop it finely, and with one deft stroke, smoothed it into a perfect, white line.

"I used to do the heavy stuff," she said. "You know, morphine, heroin. But after OD'ing twice, I learned my lesson. Needles scare the hell out of me now. And don't get me started about crack. It's *way* too addictive." She left out the part about crack-cocaine being viewed as a ghetto drug, with the powdered version for the affluent, and that at this stage in her life she felt a kinship with the latter.

She offered the straw to Aaron. "Would you like to go first?"

"Oh, you go right ahead," Aaron said. He was pretty sure he wouldn't be joining her. His experience with morphine as a pain killer was not all that wonderful, and he wasn't sure he'd fare any better using cocaine. Besides, even if he did try it, he needed to watch and learn first, so as not to appear foolish and inexperienced in front of Brandy.

She picked up the straw, and with her index finger over one nostril, she did the entire line in one quick easy motion. She tilted her head back and repeatedly sniffed and pinched her nostrils until every last grain of powder was gone.

"I never told anyone this," she confessed. "But I always wished I'd been born a blonde."

"No kidding," Aaron said, surprised at her sudden candor. "I *love* your red hair."

Brandy smiled. "Why, thank you, Aaron. What a nice thing to say."

She drew another perfect line on the mirror and handed the straw to Aaron. "Okay, big boy," she said. "Your turn."

Aaron hesitated, and then took the straw from her, feeling enormous pressure to perform. He leaned over and following Brandy's example did the line in one quick snort. The powder burned slightly, but it was nothing compared to the Jack Daniels he had coughed up through his nose that night in the van before the infamous bank robbery two years earlier. The frightful memories of that morning in the Community Plaza Bank came rushing up to his consciousness, but he quickly shoved them back down into the dark abyss where they belonged.

Brandy offered him another line, but although the sensation was most certainly pleasant, he declined. *Better see what happens to me first,* he thought wisely.

Brandy finished off the rest of the packet on her own.

"You don't talk much sometimes," she said as she repacked the little purse.

"I don't always have something to say," Aaron said.

"Do you think I'm pretty?"

Aaron adjusted his position on the bed. "Of course I do, Brandy. I'm not *blind*. Your hair, your eyes, your —"

He stopped mid-sentence when, out of the blue, Brandy crossed her arms in front of her and pulled off her top. He took in a quick breath and his eyes went wide. Brandy looked really good in black underwear.

"We can't do this, Brandy," he insisted. "You're with Jason, and he's my friend. Doesn't that matter to you?"

"Well, of course it does, silly," she said, dispatching what was left of her clothing. "Trust me. He won't mind."

"But I've never —"

Brandy pressed her finger to his lips. Her touch was soft and her skin smelled sweet and wonderful. The intoxicating cocktail of perfume, cocaine, adrenaline, and hormones heated him to his core, burning away any fragments of resistance he once had, leaving him weak.

Brandy knew she had him. She reached in and pulled his T-shirt off over his head and shoved him back onto his pillow.

She unbuttoned his jeans and as Aaron started to close his eyes, something outside caught his attention and his heart leaped. He sat up and checked the window. They were clear of the locks!

"Get dressed," he said, sitting up. "We're through the first locks. We're on Lake Gatun."

Brandy sat up with her hands covering her breasts. "What? Already? But we were just getting started."

"There's no time," Aaron said. He crawled off the bed and buttoned his pants and pulled on his shirt.

"Please don't do this," Brandy said innocently. "I can be quick."

"I'm really sorry, Brandy," Aaron said. "But Jason will be looking for you." He handed Brandy her sandals.

Dazed and embarrassed, Brandy dressed and then checked herself in the mirror. She had never been snubbed by a man before, and she didn't like the way it felt. Not one bit. Was she losing her sexuality? Did she cross some kind of line at twenty-seven? Had Aaron really *wanted* her? Or did she just imagine it all?

She made a few quick adjustments to her makeup, then gave herself a kiss in the mirror and told herself, *I'm smart enough to know when I've been insulted ... but I'm sexy enough not to care!*

As she stepped out of Aaron's cabin, she gave him a look that said, *You missed your chance, Mister. You were about to go where most men only dream of going!*

Chapter 30

Aaron watched Brandy leave, his crotch aching from the thought of what they had almost done. *I guess that mystery's going to remain a mystery*, he thought sadly. Exhausted, yet still buzzing from the cocaine, he threw back a couple of shots of Jack Daniels and lay down on his bed, and it wasn't long before he fell asleep again.

"Wake up you useless sod!" a man's voice boomed.

Aaron started and opened his eyes, frightened and confused. *Where the hell am I?* he thought, glancing around in wide-eyed panic. In the dim light he could make out what looked like the corroded bars of a cell door in a *medieval dungeon*.

The man hammered hard on the bars with what sounded like a wooden club, shattering Aaron's eardrums. "You walk at noon!" the man bellowed with the power of five men combined. Then, without another word, the man's heavy footsteps receded into the distance.

Perspiration stood in hot beads upon Aaron's forehead as ice water surged through his veins. He looked down at himself and found that he was dressed in some sort of tattered robe, woven from a coarse serge. His feet were bare and crusted with filth.

The smell of human waste hung heavily in the air, and he could see that he was indeed in some sort of dungeon. The walls were of heavy, stacked stone, glistening with moisture, and polished from centuries of human agony. Bolted to one of them was the bunk on which he sat, a wrought-iron platform supported by two heavy chains. A woven-straw mat served as his only bedding.

Above the bunk a small window was cut high into the wall. Aaron quickly determined that even if he could reach it, which he could not, it would be too narrow for him to pass through.

A thin shaft of sunlight angled down across the dank space, illuminating a small patch on the floor, revealing a swarm of roaches feeding on a scrap of something disgusting.

Aaron stood up from his bunk, but the pavers underfoot were treacherous with slime, and in the gloom he tripped on the torn hem of his robe and fell hard to the stone floor.

From his prone position, he noticed something startling: although his chest and hands were in contact with the stone, his chin and face appeared to be suspended in cold, thin air. He reached out in front of him and shuddered at finding nothing but empty space. His nostrils drew in the damp, disgusting smell of mold and decaying flesh, nearly gagging him. He spat into the darkness, waiting several seconds before hearing the faint sound of spittle hitting water. A cold thrill of terror arced up his spine. Through a stroke of pure dumb luck, he had escaped the horror of falling headlong into some sort of deep well, or pit. His malevolent captors had thoughtfully provided him more than just a bellowing thug with a club with which to facilitate his untimely doom, and he considered himself exceedingly fortunate to have avoided what he hoped was the more terrifying of the two options.

He edged back from the well, finding it difficult to maintain enough grip with his hands to regain his feet. He groped backward and grasped the chain suspending the low bunk from the wall, managing to pull himself up.

He lay back down on the mat and shut his eyes tightly, hoping to shut out the ghastly nightmare. *This can't be happening,* he cried to himself. *This can't possibly be happening!*

But every time he dared open his eyes, he was greeted by the same forbidding surroundings.

After tossing blindly on the iron bunk for what felt like hours, Aaron heard the dismal echo of heavy footsteps in the corridor.

He froze, tucking his legs up under his arms, straining to see through the bars into the corridor beyond.

KaClank!

The turnkey had unlocked the heavy lock on the cell door. He swung the iron gate wide and stepped into the narrow shaft of light. A giant of a man, the jailer stood seven feet at the shoulders, with the girth of an ox. He wore a leather vest with no shirt, revealing a massive chest soaked with sweat and crisscrossed with jagged scars. In lieu of pants he wore a rough leather kilt, held in place by a wide belt from which hung a long, straight sword and a coiled, leather whip. Legs like pier pilings ended in huge troll feet wrapped in leather.

"The sun is high," he boomed. "Come with me." He stepped into the hall and waited.

Aaron hesitated, frightfully perplexed. None of this made any sense, but strain as he may, he couldn't wake himself. Knowing of no other option but to go with the man, he stood up from the bunk, pulled up the hem of his robe, and shuffled cautiously past the pit toward the door.

Aaron followed the towering goon down a dark, narrow, stone corridor, hewn from and polished to the same smooth finish as the stone in his cell. Wrought-iron torches mounted at intervals along the way providing what little light there was.

They passed other cells, and once again the sour stench of decay filled Aaron's nostrils. Most of the cells appeared to be empty, but the ones that were occupied held sights that would chill a coroner's blood — sights that Aaron would be long to forget.

In one cell Aaron saw a nude woman with long, red hair, lying on her back strapped to an evil looking instrument of torture. As he passed, she turned her head and stared at him through blood-red eyes. Then she hissed at him, causing the hair on his neck to stand. He couldn't help but imagine what the machine was designed to do to her, but he quickly pushed the horrid image out of his mind.

In another cell Aaron saw a man sitting on the stone floor dressed in rags. He held a large knife in one hand, and it looked like he was attempting to chew his own arm off — and it appeared that he was succeeding. He looked up, and Aaron saw that his face was tattooed with a flower, but where his eyes should have been, there were only dark holes through which Aaron could see the very depths of hell.

After that Aaron kept his eyes to himself.

When at last they reached the end of the corridor, they climbed to the top of a long flight of steps. The turnkey shoved hard against a heavy door and the stairway flooded with sunlight. Aaron shaded his eyes from the painful glare, unable to see what awaited him outside.

They stepped through the door into a large courtyard of packed earth strewn with straw. The hot sun hung directly overhead.

Aaron saw a shiny new tungsten silver Aston Martin DBS parked near a stable with horses, but it meant nothing to him.

A crowd had gathered, dressed like they were attending a Renaissance festival: the men in tunics, with leather belts and feathered hats; the ladies in flowing dresses, with flowers in their hair and their bosoms mostly exposed. But it wasn't long before Aaron saw what the crowd had come to see — and it wasn't a festival.

Toward the back of the courtyard stood a large, wooden scaffold, erected from sturdy timbers with wooden stairs leading up one side. Standing on top of the raised platform, overlooking the crowd, was a large man wearing a black hood that covered his face.

"Keep moving," the jailer said gruffly, giving Aaron a hefty shove toward the scaffold.

Surely that man's not waiting for me, Aaron thought, looking around.

The crowd had grown quite large, and as he and his jailer worked their way through, Aaron was spat upon, poked with sticks, and pelted with rotten fruit. At times he thought he might faint, but the harrowing thought of being underfoot in this mob motivated him to keep moving.

When at last they reached the scaffold, the turnkey let go of Aaron's arm, indicating the stairs with a wave of his hand.

Aaron's robes were drenched with sweat and covered with muck. He looked around in disbelief. *What am I doing here?* he asked himself for the hundredth time. *Why can't I make any sense of this? Who am I, really?*

He placed his foot on the first step, and then took another step, and another, and at last he reached top of the platform.

The man in the hood directed him to kneel in front of a large block of wood with a basket sitting next to it — both were soaked with fresh blood.

The man selected a large, double-bladed axe from a rack full of such weapons. Its razor edges glinted in the sun. Aaron noticed that there was no blood on the blade. Clearly the man took pride in his work.

The axeman had Aaron rest his forehead on the block — it felt warm and sticky against his skin. He could not believe that after all he'd been through he was about to die at the hands of a medieval executioner.

"Do you have any last words?" the axeman said, his tone jaded, not at all sympathetic.

The crowd stared at Aaron expectantly, some of them no doubt pondering what *they* would say in answer to that most provocative of questions.

"No," Aaron replied. "I have nothing to say."

A round of enthusiastic booing could be heard from the crowd. Aaron knew he had disappointed them. But he really *didn't* have anything to say. What *could* he say? He had no idea why he was being executed, and he could think of nothing to give penance for.

The axeman stepped over next to the block and adjusted the position of Aaron's head so that he faced slightly to one side. To his dismay, Aaron could now see the people who had arrived early and secured the front row. Some of them had brought their children, the youngest of whom wouldn't look squarely at him; but some of the older ones were obviously getting a kick out of Aaron's dire predicament, and they had no problem making eye contact as they jeered at him with rotting teeth.

At least the guy could have given me a hood, Aaron thought bitterly.

He wanted to turn away, but he remained still, lest he not give the axeman a clean shot at his neck.

The crowd cheered wildly, feathered hats flying through the air.

Why are they in such a frenzy? Aaron thought. *What are they hoping to gain from this experience? What do they expect their kids to gain from it? Where is their compassion? Their humanity?*

The axeman rested his hand briefly on Aaron's shoulder, as if to say 'It's time.' Then a hush came over the crowd as he raised his shiny axe high overhead.

Then *WHACK!*

Aaron didn't feel a thing — his executioner was obviously an expert.

He had read somewhere that human heads lived for a few seconds after being severed, and now, flipping face first into the woven basket, and he knew that they did.

He felt strangely safe and secure in his basket. *At least I don't have to look at them*, he thought. *I'll just wait here till Death takes me away forever.*

But then, to his infinite horror, the executioner leaned down and grabbed him by the hair and lifted him out of the basket, holding him aloft, to the morbid delight of the hysterical mob. They screamed and danced in perverse ecstasy. Several women swooned and fell, only to be trampled underfoot as the crowd surged forward in a communal frenzy that had reached a fever pitch.

Aaron tried to scream, but of course he had no lungs with which to do so. He could only close his eyes and pray for a swift, sweet death.

But sadly, Death wouldn't come.

SMACK!

Aaron jerked awake and sat up holding his cheek, and for a second he was disoriented. But then he saw Brandy Fine standing in front of him and he knew he was back on the *Cayman Jewel*.

"*What did you do that for?*" he said, wishing she had brought him out of his wild dream with a bit more finesse. But then it dawned on him why she might be angry with him.

"Oh — shut up," Brandy said, disgusted. "You were flying all over the bed acting like a fucking lunatic. 'They all stare!' you said. 'Make them stop!' you said. What was I supposed to do? Bring you warm milk and a cookie? You're a grown man, Aaron. If you can't take a fucking nap after getting high without freaking out, then *forget* the damn naps. Otherwise, we're dropping you off at the next fucking nursery school!"

She walked out.

Dazed, Aaron rubbed his cheek and flopped back down on his bed, grateful to be rid of that insane dream but unable to remember a word Brandy had just said.

Chapter 31

Due to a log jam at the locks on the Pacific side, the canal crossing ended up taking two days.

Jason's canal agent said goodbye in Panama City, and at last the *Cayman Jewel* sailed out into the Pacific Ocean.

Detective Harness and his partner had waited a day and a half in Panama City, but by the time they figured out that they'd been given bad information by their own canal agent, the *Cayman Jewel* had already gone.

Jason waited until they were far from shore and then set the ship to autopilot. He joined Brandy and Aaron on the aft deck.

"Two years ago I promised you we'd marry," he said to Brandy. "Well, today's the day."

Brandy was floored. "What?"

"I wanted to wait until we made it safely through the canal," Jason said.

Brandy gave him a big hug and kiss. "Oh, Jason. I can hardly believe it!" She stopped and looked at him. "But we're miles from *anywhere*. Who will marry us?"

"I'm a ship's captain, right?" Jason said. "*I* will preside." He knew he wasn't actually qualified to marry anyone, but he figured what Brandy didn't know wouldn't hurt her.

Aaron had heard about captains marrying people and he was pretty sure it wasn't legally binding back in the States. But he'd also heard of an unwritten law that said if you truly *think* you've been married, you have, and he had no reason to believe otherwise.

Jason looked at him. "Aaron will be our witness."

"Awesome!" Aaron said, truly happy for them. "Do you have a ring?"

Jason reached into his pocket and produced a ring box with two rings and a slip of paper. He gave the rings to Aaron and faced Brandy, reading from the prepared notes.

"Do you, Brandy Fine, take me, Jason Beckham, to be your lawfully wedded husband?"

Brandy paused for a moment; it all seemed rushed and *very* unromantic, not at all what she'd dreamt it would be. She searched Jason for the faintest sign of true love, but it wasn't there. She couldn't see herself in his eyes.

The idea of marriage suddenly felt trite: the vows, the rings, the kiss. More than ever before, she deeply regretted never having had the chance to marry Johnny Souther. In spite of his faults, he had loved her truly. And she had loved him.

She began to wonder what she'd been thinking, going on this wild adventure with a man who didn't love her. And did she love Jason enough to be a good wife for him? Even if the feelings weren't mutual? She wasn't sure. But she had nowhere else to go, nothing else to live for. She may as well take a chance on being Mrs. Jason Beckham.

"I do," she said at last, adding a brief, silent prayer.

Jason gestured for her to continue.

"What? Oh — um, do you, Jason Beckham, take me, Brandy Fine, to be your lawfully wedded wife?"

She waited, smiling to herself, savoring the moment she'd yearned for her whole life.

"I do," Jason said.

Brandy searched his eyes. *Do you mean it, Jason? Is there even a small part of you that means it?*

Aaron handed them the rings and the newlyweds placed them on each other's fingers.

I will pretend that he loves me, Brandy thought. *Where is it written that I can't pretend?*

"I now pronounce us husband and wife," Jason said.

"You may kiss the bride," Aaron added.

Brandy giggled and closed her eyes again, and then she and Jason kissed.

~ PART II ~

FRIDAY
NINE DAYS LATER ...

SAN DIEGO BAY

Chapter 32

It was early afternoon on a Friday when at last Jason, Brandy, and Aaron left Mexican waters and crossed into the United States, about 3 miles offshore. The trip had taken longer than planned — with the delays in Costa Rica and Panama, and refueling issues in Cabo San Lucas — and they were running late.

They cruised a short way up the coast of California with Jason pointing out the San Diego headquarters of the U.S. Navy Seals and the Hotel Del Coronado which could be seen just east of their position, on the south side of Coronado Island.

Jason recalled a story about a famous long-time resident of the hotel: the ghost of Kate Morgan.

"I believe it was November 24th, 1892," he explained, "A woman named Kate Morgan checked into room 304, now 3327, to meet her husband ... but he never arrived. Five days later she was found dead on the steps leading to the beach. They determined she had shot herself. However, it was reported that during the coroner's inquest, the bullet found in Kate's head did not match that of her own gun — but that was never proven. And since that day, guests who have checked into room 3327 have frequently reported ghost sightings and other paranormal events."

"Remind me not to stay in *that* room," Aaron said.

"Me, too," Brandy said.

"Many famous people have stayed at the Hotel Del," Jason said. "Thomas Edison and Marilyn Monroe to name just two."

Jason prepared to sail through the entrance to San Diego Bay. "Would you like to take the helm?" he asked Aaron.

"Sure," Aaron said, surprised. Jason had never let him near the wheel this close to shore before. But he was confident he could handle it.

"Pay attention to the channel markers," Jason said. "Red, right, returning."

Aaron was familiar with the mnemonic and quickly spotted the buoys.

"The nuclear submarine base is on the west side of the channel, and North Island is to the east, to starboard," Jason said. "These are restricted areas."

"What happens if we enter a restricted area?" Brandy asked.

"They U.S. Navy will blow us out of the water," Jason said. "No questions asked."

Brandy's eyes went wide at that thought.

"Duly noted," Aaron said, and then he carefully guided the *Cayman Jewel* through the narrow channel entrance to San Diego Bay.

"That's Naval Air Station North Island to starboard, on Coronado Island. To port is Naval Base Point Loma, one of America's largest and most tactically important nuclear submarine bases. Its facilities include the Fleet Antisubmarine Warfare Training Center, Fleet Combat Training Center Pacific, and Space and Naval Warfare Systems Command, among others."

Aaron was impressed but disappointed that the awesome submarines were hidden from his view by some kind of huge floats.

"Follow the channel as it turns east," Jason said. "After Harbor Island, roughly nine nautical miles east of here, we'll jog north again. We're heading for the A-9 Cruiser Anchorage, for 'out of town' boats like ours. It'll be off your port bow, just south of the U.S. Coast Guard Station, across from the Maritime Museum of San Diego."

Aaron nodded and took them the rest of the way in.

As they approached the anchorage, they passed the MMSD on their right.

Jason pointed out one of the submarines on exhibit at the museum. "That's b-39, code name Cobra," he said. "That's why I'm here."

Brandy looked down at the 284-foot hunk of black iron moored at the dock along side the museum. "We sailed all the way here for that?" she said. The submarine had obviously seen better days and looked very unsafe.

"She's a former Soviet attack sub," Jason said. "A Foxtrot-class hunter killer. She's about to undergo a top to bottom restoration, and I've been hired as a technical consultant."

Aaron glanced down at the submarine, hoping to see it close up later. Then he concentrated on his job at the helm, carefully guiding the *Cayman Jewel* into the anchorage.

Jason tied up at a mooring buoy and joined the others on deck. "Talk about cutting it close," he said, checking his watch. "It's 3:45 p.m. I'm scheduled to meet Uri Ruden on board Cobra at 4:00."

He looked at Aaron. "Captain Ruden is one of the Russian submariners who actually piloted Cobra during the Cold War back in the Seventies. Would you like to meet him and check out the sub?"

"Hell, yeah," Aaron said.

Jason turned to Brandy. "The mooring office will be expecting us to contact them for an inspection and a permit. Their phone number is up on the chart table. We shouldn't be long."

Brandy nodded. She was happy to stay behind and relax on deck while the men had their fun.

San Diego Waterfront

Chapter 33

Jason and Aaron lowered the *Cayman Jewel's* dinghy, an 18-foot Zodiac inflatable outboard, into the water and motored across the basin to the MMSD. At 4 p.m. sharp, they walked up Cobra's gangway to meet Uri Ruden.

"Welcome to San Diego," Uri said, shaking Jason's hand firmly. "I trust your trip was a pleasurable one."

Jason hesitated then decided not to mention the pirate attack that almost ended their voyage. "It was a relaxing cruise, thank you. Uneventful."

He gestured toward Aaron. "Uri, this is my good friend Aaron Quinn. Aaron, meet Captain Third Rank, Uri Ruden, a former Soviet submariner. Uri is here to help whip Cobra into shape."

Aaron couldn't imagine what Jason meant by "whip Cobra into shape", as if that were even possible. He stepped forward and shook Ruden's hand. "Pleased to meet you, Captain," he said.

"You as well, Mr. Quinn," Uri said.

"Aaron's a SCUBA instructor down on Cayman Brac," Jason said. "He's an accomplished sailor himself and owns his own boat. He crewed for me on our trip up here — very capably, I might add."

Uri guessed Aaron to be about eighteen. "Captain Pankov's daughter will be happy to know she won't be the only person under twenty at the welcome party tonight," he said.

Jason had heard about the party, but he hadn't planned on having Aaron hanging around while he and his fellow conspirators conducted business. Uri obviously wasn't concerned, though, so he let it go.

"I wasn't aware that Pankov had a daughter," he said.

"He does indeed," Uri said. "She's his only child, and with her father's Russian good looks and a beautiful Korean mother, Ekatarina Vtorakevna Pankova isn't a woman you'll easily forget."

Jason and Aaron tried to picture her ethnic blend but couldn't.

Aaron was stoked to be invited to the welcome party. He had no idea who Captain *Pankov* was, but he would definitely check out the man's daughter. He liked the way the name *Ekatarina* rolled off his tongue.

"Are the Pankovs here yet?" Jason asked.

"I believe Ekatarina arrived yesterday," Uri said. "However, Captain Pankov had last minute business to attend to back in Russia, and he's due in later tonight. Fagan should be here around 7:00."

Jason was curious to see Ekatarina's beautiful Korean mother. "And Pankov's wife?"

"Mrs. Pankov succumbed to breast cancer four years ago," Uri said.

"I'm sorry," Jason said.

Uri knew that Pankov had never fully recovered from the loss of his wife, and that it was one of the reasons the old Captain was losing his mind; but he didn't mention it.

"Perhaps while we're waiting we could explore this beautiful, once top-secret combat submarine?" he said, indicating the b-39.

Jason checked his watch. 4:05 p.m. "You'll have to pardon me, Captain," he said, "but I have another appointment. Perhaps Aaron would appreciate a tour."

Uri looked at Aaron expectantly.

"I'd love it," Aaron said. He had never seen the inside a real submarine before.

"I'll be back in time for the party," Jason said and excused himself.

Chapter 34

"We'll begin topside and then go below," Uri said, "working our way from bow to stern."

"Sounds good," Aaron said.

"It takes years of specialized training to understand the operations of an attack sub," Uri said, "but I'll try and whittle it down. Let me know if I go too fast, as I wouldn't want you to get lost during the party."

Aaron laughed. "That would *not* be good," he said. He was serious about meeting Ekatarina.

Uri gestured toward a heavy, flat-steel hoop about 3 feet in diameter mounted vertically on the dock near the gangway. "Do you see that big ring mounted there?" he said.

Aaron nodded.

"That's a mock-up of one of b-39's watertight hatches, or bulkhead doors. The maritime museum installed it so visitors can see if they can fit through Cobra's real hatches. They don't want anyone getting stuck inside their submarine."

"I hate when that happens," Aaron said, grinning.

He turned to give the mock-up a try. He had to stoop very low, but he managed to step through easily.

"Try doing that in a hurry with eighty other men in flooded conditions while under attack," Uri said.

"I can't even imagine," Aaron said. Then he followed Uri up a ramp onto Cobra's main deck.

"What you see when you look at a submarine is just a skin, or shell, which floods with seawater when submerged," Uri explained. "The skin gives the sub its streamlined shape and helps protect the vital inner hull, or pressure hull, from damage. Like a space capsule, the pressure hull is the main component of the crew's life support system, and if it is breached, or punctured, things can go bad in a hurry."

Aaron looked around at Cobra's heavy, steel-plated skin, painted a dull black.

"Within the pressure hull there are a total of seven compartments," Uri went on, "lined up end to end, with one long, narrow corridor running through them — just like you would see on a passenger train. Compartment One is up in the bow, followed by Compartments Two, Three, and Four, and so on down the line, ending with Compartment Seven in the stern."

"That's a lot of compartments," Aaron said.

"Yes, and many of the main compartments house smaller compartments," Uri said. "It may sound confusing, but actually the layout is very simple: Compartment One is the Forward Torpedo Room, Cobra's primary weapon array, and the main reason for an attack sub like her to exist. Compartment Two contains the Captain's Cabin, the Sonar Room, other Officer's Quarters, and the Officer's Ward Room. Compartment Three houses the Control Center, otherwise known as the Control Room — the heart and brain of the sub. Compartment Four houses Midshipmen's Quarters and the galley. Compartments Five and Six are the Engine Room, and the Electric Motor Room, respectively. And finally, Compartment Seven, in the stern, contains the Aft Torpedo Room."

"Where are the hatches that trap tourists?" Aaron asked.

"Four of these seven compartments are considered vital," Uri explained, "and they are secured by watertight hatches which can be sealed off from the rest of the submarine in the event the main pressure hull is compromised. The first vital space is Compartment Two, with watertight hatches at each end — one leading to Compartment One and the other leading to Compartment Three."

Aaron counted two hatches on his fingers.

"Compartments Four, Five, and Six, are also considered vital, and similar to Compartment Two, they actually grouped into a single module with watertight hatches at each end."

"One leading to Compartment Three and one to Compartment Seven," Aaron said, picturing it easily now.

"Correct," Uri said. "The crew could move from one end of the sub to the other along the main corridor using just those four hatches."

"Let me see if I've got this straight," Aaron said. "If the pressure hull fails, the corridor running through the seven compartments can be cordoned off as needed using four watertight hatches, as a last defense against the incoming seawater."

"Precisely," Uri said. "But there are more hatches here on deck. For instance the hatch toward the bow, used to load torpedoes into the Forward Torpedo Room with a crane from above, and the escape hatch above Compartment Seven, the Aft Torpedo Room, toward the stern. The fin hatch, here amidships, provides access to the ladder leading to the Control Room in Compartment Three. Think of it as Cobra's main entrance. I'll point it out later. Are you ready to go below?"

"Ready," Aaron said.

They walked past Cobra's large, black fin and continued on toward the bow, stopping at a steep, narrow set of steel stairs leading down into the sub's dark interior.

"These bow stairs were cut through what used to be the torpedo loading hatch I mentioned earlier," Uri said.

"Above the Forward Torpedo Room," Aaron said.

"Yes, Compartment One," Uri agreed. "We submariners didn't have the luxury of these stairs. We entered the boat through the fin hatch using the ladder to the Control Room. These and most of the handrails and ramps you see on deck were installed by the maritime museum for the benefit of the public. But since they're here, why not use them. Follow me."

Aaron and Uri descended the tourist stairs into the Forward Torpedo Room.

"Foxtrots were armed with high explosive torpedoes with a range of ten miles," Uri said. "The weapons could be fired from six forward, or four aft 533 millimeter or 21-inch torpedo tubes. You're looking at the six forward tubes."

Aaron could not believe the amount of equipment crammed into such a tight space.

He saw what reminded him of a World War I gas mask hanging from a hook. "Is that for if the air in here goes bad?" he asked, pointing at the odd looking device.

"You're close," Uri said. "It's actually a Submerged Escape Apparatus. In other words, a lung, for breathing underwater during an escape." He took it off the hook and handed it to Aaron.

Aaron turned the contraption over in his hands. It consisted of a rubber lung, a steel bottle, a mouthpiece, and goggles. "How does it work?" he asked.

"It combines a CO2 scrubber with supplemental oxygen to hopefully provide enough breathable air for an escapee to make it to the surface." Uri said. "The museum hung it here, along with other memorabilia, to add realism. That one's pretty old, though. The scrubbing canister's probably shot, and I doubt there's much oxygen left in the bottle. I never had to use one, thank God."

Aaron hung the lung back on its hook.

"A submarine torpedo tube is like a large naval gun," Uri said. "It's basically a barrel with a breech and muzzle. However, a torpedo tube uses compressed air rather than an explosive for the purpose of firing, and the tube's projectile is self-propelling, the tube supplying only the initial boost for the torpedo."

He indicated one of the heavy torpedo racks. "When fully armed, Cobra carried twenty-two torpedoes. These are two of them."

Aaron stepped over to take a closer look at the huge, colorful bombs, both over 20-feet long. One of the weapons was painted fire-engine red, with white stripes. It was shaped like a cigar, like the torpedoes he had seen in pictures.

The second torpedo, however, looked quite different: it was painted forest green and was at least two feet longer than the other. It was tipped with an articulating nosecone made of brightly polished metal, and looked much sleeker, faster, and deadlier than its counterpart.

"These torpedoes have been disarmed of course," Uri said. "Would you like to see how they're loaded?"

"Sure," Aaron said. He had always wondered how that was done.

"The gantry crane is used to move the rack and align a specific torpedo with the tube," Uri said. "Then the pulley system pulls the weapon in."

He craned the rack over and loaded the red and white torpedo into tube 5. "Did you get how that was done?" he said.

"I think so," Aaron said.

Uri withdrew the bomb and settled it back onto the rack. "Go ahead, try loading the green torpedo into tube five."

Aaron followed Uri's instructions and loaded the weapon, and then he reached up to close the tube's inner hatch cover.

"You can leave the hatch cover open," Uri said. "I'll secure everything later. Let's move on to Compartment Two."

Compartment Two was accessed through the first of the four watertight hatches along the main corridor. Uri led the way and Aaron ducked in behind him. The corridor was very tight, leaving barely enough room for two men to squeeze past each other.

"Daily life was on a three-shift schedule," Uri said. "On duty, maintenance, sleep. The first door on your right is the Captain's Cabin, followed by the Sonar Room and a four-berth Officer's Cabin. Only we officers had our own bunks. Enlisted men hot bunked."

"What's *hot bunked*?" Aaron said.

"Fifty four crewmen sharing 27 bunks located in the Electric Motor Room and the Aft Torpedo Room," Uri said.

Aaron peeked into the various cabins, each with its own thin wood door. He was amazed by how small they all were

— he'd been spoiled by the generous accommodations on the *Cayman Jewel*.

Uri pointed out a tiny conference room with enough space for about six officers tightly packed. "The last room, here in Compartment Two, is the Officer's Ward Room," he said. "A Zampolit, or Soviet Political Officer, was assigned to every submarine. He also quartered here in Compartment Two, near the Commander, and near to any meetings held here. Usually a Captain Third Rank, his sole task was enforcing adherence to Communist Party doctrine."

They continued on, passing through the second watertight hatch and into Compartment Three.

"This is the Control Center," Uri said. "The nerve center of the submarine."

He pointed to a ladder a short distance away. "That's the main ladder leading up to the fin hatch, the hatch to the bridge. It also leads to the periscope viewing compartment. The periscope was normally not accessible from here in the Control Room, but for safety reasons the conning tower is not open to tourists, so the attack periscope's well was cut away to permit access at this level."

Uri had taken that into consideration when calculating the team's minimum manpower requirements.

Aaron looked up the ladder into the fin longingly.

"There in the corner is one of only two heads on board," Uri said, pointing to a small open door in the corner of the Control Room. "Two toilets and one shower served 80 or so officers and enlisted men for up to three months at sea. Lingering in the head was considered a crime against humanity, and the men often used the ship's flooded areas as convenient latrines."

"Wow," Aaron said, and then he followed Uri through the third watertight hatch into Compartment Four.

Uri showed Aaron the Radio Room and the Midshipmen's Cabin. Next came the pantry and the tiny galley, a space barely large enough for two short cooks to stand. To Aaron the galley looked like an afterthought, which seemed weird, considering the importance of food.

"The chef and his assistants prepared four meals a day here," Uri said. "Menus were chosen by the Supply Officer and the Chef a week in advance and approved by the Captain. The Captain and Supply Officer also tasted all meals served at dinner and supper to ensure they met the required standard. Officers down through seamen ate the same menu. Chefs were highly prized by submarine captains, because good food meant a happy crew, and Russian submariners enjoyed the best food in the Soviet Navy.

"A typical day would have been breakfast at 7:00, consisting of coffee, bread, cheese, eggs, sausage or bacon. Dinner, midday, was soup or borscht, meat with rice or noodles, or goulash, salad or vegetables. Dinner also included a half a glass of white wine, but they would have much preferred the officially banned vodka that the officers enjoyed. Supper came at around 6:00, with soup, meat with rice or noodles, a soft drink or juice, a chocolate bar, salted fish, tea, caviar, and fruit. Tea followed at 10:00, with cookies or pancakes or piroschki."

"Piroschki?" Aaron said.

"It's a type of pie," Uri said. "Rations for three months were loaded on the boat at the beginning of a patrol, with all available space used for food storage. Officers dined in the Ward Room and the seamen on fold out tables in various corners of the boat. Food scraps were disposed of through a small tube in the galley which fired the refuse into the sea just like a torpedo."

Aaron pictured schools of fish hanging out by the discharge tube, like underwater seagulls waiting for scraps.

They descended the small set of stairs leading to Compartment Five, the Machinery Control and Engine Rooms.

"Cobra has three Kolomna 2D24M Turbo Diesel Engines that produce 2,000 horsepower each," Uri explained, "driving the submarine at up to 8 knots with a maximum range of 20,000 nautical miles. The diesels charge batteries that drive the electric motors in Compartment Six, and the boat can run on either — similar to how a hybrid automobile like the Prius operates. It is essentially the same thing — very quiet when running on battery power."

They checked out Compartment Six, the Electric Motor Room, and then ducked through the last watertight hatch into Compartment Seven, the Aft Torpedo Room.

Uri wrapped up the tour by showing Aaron the four aft torpedo tubes and pointing out a few of the crew's tiny shared berths.

"That was fascinating," Aaron said. "It must be quite an adventure going underwater in one of these."

"Trust me, it is," Uri said. "Perhaps you'll get a chance to dive in one yourself someday."

"That would be amazing," Aaron said, thinking, *Like that'll ever happen. Only VIPs get those opportunities.*

Uri pointed to a second set of tourist stairs leading out through the overhead bulkhead. "Those stairs lead up to the deck," he said. "Why don't you head out and take a look around the waterfront. San Diego's really very beautiful."

"I'll do that," Aaron said, and he meant it. This was his first and probably last time in San Diego, and he planned to take advantage of it.

They shook hands and Aaron started up the stairs.

"Don't forget about the welcome party," Uri said after him.

"Oh, I won't," Aaron said over his shoulder. He was still counting on meeting Ekatarina.

When Aaron emerged from the aft stairway, he was surprised to see that a construction crew had arrived and were busily erecting a large, white-plastic tent, no doubt intending to cover the submarine entirely. *Must have to do with Jason's restoration work*, he thought, as he made his way through the debris.

As he stepped off Cobra's gangway onto the dock, Aaron noticed a sign promoting the Maritime Museum of San Diego gift shop, and since it was located right next door, he decided to check it out.

Chapter 35

The museum gift shop was stocked with books on sailing, local history, and folklore, along with nautically themed gifts, and beautifully framed photos of famous sailing ships and explorers.

Aaron couldn't help but notice the cute brunette, about eighteen or nineteen, working behind the counter. She wore a baby-blue MMSD T-shirt, white yachting shorts, and a narrow belt that matched her top. When she reached for an item on a high shelf, the T-shirt tugged at her firm breasts, and Aaron found it impossible not to stare.

He stopped and pretended to look at some items in a glass case across the room from her.

"So, what brings you to the Maritime Museum?" the young woman asked, surprising him.

"Oh — hi," he stammered, looking up. "I-I'm just here to see the Russian submarine."

She glanced out the window and saw that construction of the tarpaulin was well under way. "I'm afraid Cobra's going to be closed for maintenance for a couple of days."

"Actually, I just finished a tour," Aaron said.

"Oh, really?" the girl said.

"Yeah, a friend of mine is part of the team that's consulting on the restoration project," Aaron said. "One of the sub's former officers was kind enough to show me around."

"What a coincidence," the girl said. "My father was hired as a consultant as well. He used to be the submarine's captain. Sadly, his mind is not what it used to be, and I think he believes he's coming here to sail her again."

Aaron was too enamored of the girl to hear what she had just said. He stared into the gift case not knowing what else to say to her.

The young woman paused and looked at him. There was something compelling about him, and talking with him, in spite of being a little awkward, was surprisingly pleasant. She found herself wanting to know more about him.

She walked over and pointed out a simple, pearl necklace. "That would be the perfect gift for your girlfriend," she said, resting her hand on his forearm.

Aaron's heart did a double-beat. Her features were even more exquisite up close, and her touch was soft and warm, sending a wave of desire surging through him.

"What? Oh — I'm not seeing anyone," he said awkwardly. His recent *affaire de coeur* in the Panama Canal with Brandy Fine came to mind, but he knew better than to elevate that brief interlude to anything higher than an aborted fling with a frustrated woman.

The girl lifted her hand from Aaron's arm, appearing suddenly distant and a little sad. "I had a boyfriend back home," she confessed, thinking of him. "We had hoped to be married, but my father strongly disapproved, using every conceivable excuse to keep us apart. And now that I'm here in the United States, all *alone*, it appears his wish has come true."

"You're here alone?" Aaron asked, surprised.

"My father promised we would come to America together," she said, then added gloomily, "But I guess I was wrong to believe it was fitting for a man of his stature to travel with his *daughter*."

She paused, brightening a little. "I'm Ekatarina, by the way."

Aaron's jaw dropped. "Wait a second ... You're Captain Pankov's daughter?" Her accent made sense now.

"Why, yes," she said. "How did you know that?"

He couldn't remember. "I'm not sure," he said.

She offered him her hand expectantly, "Pleased to meet you —"

"It's Quinn, Aaron Quinn," he said, returning her handshake. "It's Irish."

Don't be such a loser! he told himself. *Ask the girl out.*

Ekatarina was thinking along the same lines. "If you're around later, there's a welcome party on the submarine tonight at 7:00."

"I heard," Aaron said stupidly.

"Are you planning on going?"

"I think so," he said. "Most likely."

Am I wasting my time here? she thought. *Are you really that clueless? Or is it just my imagination?*

"Then I guess I'll see you there," she said.

Make a move, you wuss! Aaron told himself. *Don't let her walk away!*

He coughed once and swallowed hard, bracing himself for rejection. "I-I was thinking," he said at last. "I have the Zodiac tied up outside, and well, we have a little time before the party. Would you care to join me for a quick cruise around the bay?"

The image of Boris sitting alone back home popped into Ekatarina's head again, but to her surprise, this time she had no problem clearing it away.

"I'd love to," she said, a little too quickly, and tried to slow it down. "I've been here two whole days and I haven't had a chance to see *anything*. I'll put together things for a picnic."

Aaron checked his watch. 4:45 p.m. He hadn't noticed how hungry he was, but now that she had mentioned it, he was *starving*.

Suddenly Ekatarina remembered she had to work late. "I don't get off until 5:30, if that's okay."

"Not a problem," Aaron said cheerfully. "I'll meet you on the dock."

He turned to leave, walking on air.

POINT LOMA

Chapter 36

Jason's taxi dropped him off in front of a fabulous Tudor-style house along one of the narrow, winding streets in the exclusive Point Loma hills above San Diego Bay. He walked up a brick path bordered with moss-covered stones under a thick canopy of luscious greenery.

Fagan greeted him at the door and invited him into an expanse of hardwood floors, fine leather furniture, and antique rugs.

"May I offer you a drink, my friend?" Fagan said.

"You read my mind," Jason said. "Scotch rocks, thank you. Nice place you have here." Fagan had moved up in the world since Jason had left the Navy.

Jason stepped into a living room that offered a stunning view of San Diego Bay and the sparking blue Pacific Ocean beyond. The sun was sinking low in the western sky, turning the ocean a bright pink.

He stopped next to a framed photo on the fireplace mantel: a black-and-white portrait of an exquisitely beautiful woman in her mid-to-late thirties.

"Who's the pretty lady?" he asked, indicating the photo.

"Oh, that would be Martha, my girlfriend," Fagan replied from the kitchen.

"You were always the one who got the girls," Jason said, only half kidding.

Fagan smiled. "What can I say? Some of us have it and some of us don't."

Jason walked over and stood next to the large windows overlooking the bay, far below him. Toward the south, in the distance, the sun reflected on the waters surrounding Naval Base Point Loma. Jason could just make out the dark shapes of the nuclear submarines docked there.

Fagan returned with drinks and the two sat in the living room.

"You never told me you were seeing someone," Jason said.

"Martha and I met in a bar a couple of years ago, in a small town on the East Coast. She had recently been in a serious car accident, and although she wasn't seriously injured, she was pretty messed up mentally. I guess her only son was in the car and was killed. When I met her she didn't even know her real name. She'd started drinking a lot, so I cleaned her up and named her Martha and brought her out to San Diego, hoping a fresh start would help."

He took a sip of his drink. "She'll be my guest tonight at the party. I'll make it a point to introduce you."

"You do that," Jason said.

"You seeing anyone?" Fagan said.

"Yeah."

"Is it serious?"

"Not really."

The conversation quickly turned to the details of the mission.

"The crew have already started on the security tarpaulin," Fagan said. "They should have it completed in a few hours."

"I assume they're removing all of the temporary public access equipment," Jason said.

"Of course. Tourist walkways, decking, handrails ... all gone. They will weld up any holes in the deck and pressure hull that were cut for temporary stairs, and they're charging Cobra's batteries as well."

"Sounds like you've thought this through pretty well," Jason said.

"As I'm sure you have, Jason," Fagan said. "That's what we do, right? We are trained to think."

There was a knock at the door.

"That will be Captain Henk Zaane," Fagan said, "from the cruise ship *Neau Islander*. I asked him to join us so you two could meet."

He stood and started for the door. "After this I have to head down to North Island to do my VIP greeting," he said, then added over his shoulder, "I'd ask you to ride along, but we both know you'd never get through security."

Jason flipped him off.

Fagan greeted Captain Zaane at the door and they joined Jason in the living room.

"How do you do, Jason?" Captain Zaane said. "I am excited to finally meet the man I've heard so much about."

Jason had to presume that Zaane was the fifth team member that Fagan had alluded to during breakfast back in Coronado. "And I you, Captain," he said.

They shook hands.

"If this mission is successful," Zaane said, "it will send a clear message to the Imperialist United States that the Russian nation is once again a force to be reckoned with, a world power, and that retaliation of any kind would be an exercise in futility."

Jason listened politely, but none of that really interested him. He was only in it for the money.

Just then Fagan's girlfriend pulled into the driveway. There were no cars around, so she had no way of knowing that they had visitors. She parked the car and took her groceries around to the back.

She entered the kitchen through the back door, and as she set the bags on the counter she couldn't help but overhear Fagan talking to someone in the living room.

Fagan quickly brought Jason and Captain Zaane up to speed, giving them all of the relevant details of the mission. Jason was careful not to show his surprise upon hearing for the first time that the target of the assassination was the President of the United States.

"... and at that point we move out from under your wake," Fagan said to Zaane, "and you and your guests simply cruise on out to sea, as if nothing had happened. We will remain submerged, hiding Cobra under the bait barges near Ballast Point, while we wait for our target."

"Perfect," Zaane said. "They will be totally unaware."

Fagan checked his watch then stood and proposed a simple toast. "To our success."

"*To our success,*" the men echoed. They clinked glasses and threw back their drinks.

Fagan showed his guests to the door and they all shook hands.

"I'll call you with the exact departure times," Fagan said to Zaane.

Zaane nodded, and he and Jason turned to leave.

Fagan closed the door and turned to see Martha standing in the living room, hands on her hips.

"What was *that* all about?" she asked.

"Some friends stopped by is all. Nothing important."

"Jason Souther was here."

Fagan knew he was busted. "Okay ... so what?"

"You promised me he'd never set foot in our house *again*," Martha demanded.

"*That* you remember," Fagan mumbled under his breath.

"*What?*"

Fagan's comment had obviously struck a nerve and he knew he shouldn't have gone there. "He was here for ten lousy minutes," he said quickly.

"I don't care if it was *thirty seconds*," Martha said. "We agreed, did we not? Associating with someone who got kicked out of the Navy for going *AWOL* might be detrimental to your career as an *officer*."

"Stop being so melodramatic," Fagan said. "You've never even met the man."

"What's that got to do with anything? *You're* the one who said he was trouble, and that you never wanted to see him again!"

"That was before I knew why he went AWOL!" Fagan barked.

"What are you *talking* about?" Martha said, more confused than ever.

Fagan knew he had already said too much. "Forget it," he said. "I'm going to take a shower. We'll talk about this later." He turned to leave the room.

Tears welled in Martha's eyes. "I suppose if you wanted me to know about your plot to kill the President you would have told me?" she said after him.

Fagan stopped in his tracks. She had heard everything. *Damn it! How could I be so fucking stupid!* He looked back at her, eyes flat. "I suggest you start getting cleaned up as well, Martha. I'm expecting you to be ready when I return from North Island. In case you've forgotten, we have a party to attend."

While Martha was out she had purchased a new dress and shoes for the occasion, but now she'd feel stupid putting them on. "I'm not so sure I want to go," she said, her eyes moist.

Fagan's eyes narrowed even more and he said, "Oh, you're going all right. I think it's time you and Jason Souther met."

North Island Naval Air Station
Coronado Island

Chapter 37

Air Force One dropped below the clouds, approaching San Diego from the east, and touched down on the east-west runway at Naval Air Station North Island on Coronado Island. The pilot taxied to a stop in a specially designated area of the tarmac, and the jet's wheel chocks were set and air stairs driven into place. A parade of black limousines pulled up nearby in precision formation, followed by the rolling out of the red carpet.

Soon the massive Boeing VC-25's forward passenger door opened and the President of the United States and his entourage walked down the steps to the sound of a Navy marching band.

There to greet the President were a crowd of military officers and officials.

One of the officers was Commander Richard Fagan.

Fagan stepped forward and shook hands with the President.

"Welcome to San Diego, Mr. President," Fagan said. "I'm Commander Richard Fagan of the United States Navy. It is a privilege to be your escort today. I trust you had a good flight."

"Thank you, Commander, it's good to be here," the President said.

"We've arranged for you to relax in your room for a while if your schedule permits," Fagan said.

"I'd like that," the President said. "The flight over was nothing but back to back meetings, and I could use some peace and quiet."

One of the suits charged with protecting the President wore a baby-blue carnation in his lapel. He stepped over and took Fagan aside.

"For obvious reasons, the Secret Service refuses to allow the Chief Executive to stay in a room at or near the top of a hotel," he said with a tone of arrogance.

Fagan had always hated the way these glorified security guards talked to distinguished military officers such as himself. "Thank you, Agent," he said. "I'm well aware of that policy."

He turned back to the President. "In recent years the Presidential Suite at the Hotel Del Coronado has become more a symbol of the office than a potential presidential stopover, sir. We have arranged for you to rest at what we call the *Baby Del*, a beautiful, private residence here on Coronado Island. It is totally safe and secure. Not even *I* know where it is."

"Well done, Commander," the President said. "I'm sure it will more than suit my needs."

The agent with the carnation stepped back a half step and adjusted his tie.

"In honor of your visit to San Diego, I have arranged a special VIP treat for you, Mr. President," Fagan said.

"And what might that be?" the President asked. He had already been briefed regarding his schedule for the day, but hearing it from the officer in charge was more reliable.

"Later this evening, you will board the nuclear submarine, USS *Hampton*," Fagan said. "Then, at precisely 9:00 p.m. local time, you will sail out to sea from Point Loma to observe an Emergency Nighttime Surface Drill." He pictured the dark shadow of Cobra waiting silently under the bait barges, its live torpedo cocked and loaded.

The President had heard of the exercise. "Is that where the sub shoots up out of the water like a breaching whale?" he asked candidly.

"Yes, sir," Fagan said. "It's a rare privilege, and one of the more exciting events to experience on board an attack sub — outside of combat, that is."

The agent with the carnation gave Fagan a look that said, *You Naval Officers think you're so fucking cool ...*

"Sounds like fun," the President said.

"Oh, it will be, sir," Fagan said, thinking of the real reason the President's sub was going to shoot out of the water. "I can almost guarantee you'll never forget it." He paused to look at his watch. "Unfortunately, I have other pressing business, so I won't be joining you this evening. I'll see you tomorrow at breakfast."

He and the President shook hands.

"Enjoy the ride," Fagan said, and with a quick nod to the agent with the flower, he excused himself and returned to his home on Point Loma.

San Diego Bay

Chapter 38

At just after 5:30 p.m., Aaron hopped in the Zodiac and headed across the anchorage to the MMSD. He could see Ekatarina waving at him from the dock.

The newly acquainted couple toured the bay for a while, taking in the sights, checking out the spectacular downtown San Diego skyline.

Aaron steered the Zodiac under the Coronado Bridge and into Glorietta Bay, on the east side of Coronado Island near the Hotel Del Coronado.

He asked Ekatarina to brace herself, and then he ran the small rubber craft up on the sand in a secluded area of the beach.

They unloaded their gear and carried it up onto the grass. Aaron spread out the soft blanket Ekatarina had brought, and she placed the picnic basket and some beach towels in one corner.

A steady, cool breeze blew in off the water as they sat and watched the sun going down behind the hotel.

"Where did you get that scar?" Ekatarina asked, referring to the jagged line running down Aaron's left cheek.

Aaron touched his hand to his face, unsure what to say. Then he decided to tell her the whole story: about how he had met a writer named Michael St. John, and how Michael's novel *Saturday Night Crash* had been turned into a successful movie, and how he'd been working on a sequel.

He told her how, after knowing each other for only three days, Michael had become like a father to him — the father he had yearned for ever since he was nine-years-old and his real father died in combat.

He told her about those three horrific days: the two eccentric thugs, Needles and Beeks; and the deadly bank robbery, and how when he had tried to stop it, Johnny Souther shot him.

"As if that weren't enough," he said at last, "and after all we'd been through together, at the end of the third day I lost my mother, my best friend, and Michael St. John to a hit-and-run driver."

Ekatarina looked at him in disbelief. "You poor thing," she said. "I don't know what to say."

Aaron finished by telling her about the kind detective who had found him after the crash and saved his life. "If it weren't for Detective Harness," he said, "I doubt I'd be alive today."

She could see that Aaron had been severely traumatized. She took his hand and held it gently. "It was wrong for me to ask," she said. "Perhaps we should talk about something else."

She opened the picnic basket and pulled out a peach, taking a generous bite that sent peach juice running down her chin. "Oops," she said, catching the drips with her hand.

Aaron reached over and gently wiped her mouth with a napkin, making her smile.

"What do you do for work?" she asked.

"Until recently I was down in the Cayman Islands working as a dive instructor. But like Michael St. John, my passion is writing. I hope to finish my first novel someday. I've been at it off and on for years, but something always seems to come up that keeps me from writing."

"I'd love to read something you've written sometime," Ekatarina said.

Aaron remembered an item he'd been carrying in his pocket since he left the Cayman's. He hadn't intended to ever show it to anyone, but the moment seemed right. He pulled it out and handed it to her.

"What's this?" she said.

"It's nothing really ... just a little five-by-five I wrote back in the Caymans."

"A what?"

"A complete short story in twenty-five words," Aaron explained. "Five sentences long with exactly five words per sentence."

Intrigued, Ekatarina unfolded the little piece of paper.

Hastily scratched in pencil were the following five lines:

"What troubles you, My Lady?"
"They all stare," I replied.
He shifted, blocking their view.
I smiled at the man.
He let the axe fall.

Ekatarina took a moment to absorb the full meaning of the short story. "I love it. It's a bit dark, but I love it. How can you say so much in just twenty five words?"

"Hemingway once wrote a complete story in just six words," Aaron said.

"'For sale: baby shoes, never worn.'"

Ekatarina had to consider that story for a moment as well. "Deep," she said at last. "If I didn't know you better, I'd say you and Hemingway were really screwed up."

Aaron laughed. "And you would be correct," he admitted.

Ekatarina took another big bite of her peach, controlling the juice with her napkin this time.

"What do you look for in a woman?" she asked.

Aaron paused, the random question catching him a little off guard. "Oh, I guess I don't really care ... as long as she's sweet, and pretty, and funny, and a little naughty, and smart, and loving, and a loyal friend, and —"

"So what you're trying to say is, you aren't picky," Ekatarina said, laughing.

"Precisely," Aaron said.

"Let's take a swim," Ekatarina said cheerfully, jumping to her feet. "We can pretend we're on a deserted island."

"What? Uh — I didn't bring a suit," Aaron said awkwardly.

"Neither did I, silly. Come on. No one's around ..."

Just like that she stood and kicked off her sandals and pulled off her shorts and top, leaving nothing but her bra and panties. Aaron's eyes widened at the sight of her slender, perfect body, her breasts straining to be free of their restraints, the setting sun adding a soft, sensuous glow to her smooth skin.

She waded out a bit and gestured for him to follow. "Come on in, the water's fine," she said, laughing at herself for using that tired Hollywood cliché.

Aaron looked around and then stripped to his boxers and followed her into the pristine waters of Glorietta Bay.

Ekatarina watched him, grinning widely, splashing the clear water with her fingers.

Up to mid-thigh now, she dunked under for a moment, and when she surfaced she turned toward Aaron, and, pretending not to notice that her underwear had become see-through, did a full body stretch, arms overhead, arching her back, wringing the seawater from her long, straight black hair as the salty liquid dripped from her invisible bra and shimmered down over her smooth stomach and legs.

Aaron swallowed hard, thinking, *Oh my God, am I dreaming?*

He quickly dunked under as well, hoping to extinguish the conspicuous fire Ekatarina had ignited in him. She was kidding about it being warm.

"It's *freezing*," he said, laughing, clutching his arms to his chest.

As a trained diver, Aaron could easily hold his breath for long periods, and he decided to play a harmless trick on her. He waded out a little and then dunked under again, and this time instead of surfacing right away, he stayed down for a while — a long while.

Ekatarina watched the ripples rolling away from where he'd been, the concern in her eyes deepening. He was staying down way too long. A myriad of potential aquatic horrors flashed before her eyes as she looked around for him.

Suddenly Aaron surfaced, splashing her playfully, laughing at his childish prank.

She splashed him back hard. *"Don't do that!"* she said. *"You scared me."* She didn't mention that her younger brother, her only sibling, had drowned in a canal at the age of eight, and that she had been the one that found him. She gave Aaron a shove that nearly knocked him over. Then she ran giggling out of the water and up onto the grass where she flopped onto her stomach on the picnic blanket.

Aaron walked up the beach, wiping the excess water from his chest and arms, and sat down next to her. Her cute bottom was clearly one of her best features.

The sun was very low now, and the air was cooling. Goosebumps were forming on Ekatarina's skin. Aaron reached for a towel and laid it over her, and then he grabbed one for himself and dried his hair with a quick buff.

He reached into the picnic basket and pulled out an apple. "I appreciate you putting this nice picnic together, Ekatarina."

"You're very welcome." She sat up and pulled the towel around her, covering her body entirely. Then she turned her head slightly to the side and smiled at him in a way that made his heart leap. "You know, Aaron ... in Russia it is customary for lovers to refer to each other by an affectionate name."

Aaron paused, confused. *Did I hear her right? Did she say 'lovers'? Please tell me she said 'lovers'.*

"Mine's Katya," she said. "And you already have yours."

Before Aaron could say anything, Katya pushed him gently down onto the blanket. She dropped her towel and reached behind her back and unclasped her wet bra and tossed it over her shoulder. Then she lay over him with her breasts on his chest and pressed her warm, moist lips firmly against his.

At first her directness embarrassed him, but he let himself go, bathing in her intoxicating sexuality, responding passionately to her open-mouthed kisses as if he knew he would die tomorrow. He wanted to be in this moment forever — just the two of them — spinning through space and time, safe in their dream, safe from a world gone mad. Nothing else existed, nothing else mattered. *Please, God,* he prayed.

Let this be my moment. Let this be my life. Let this be my eternity.

Her goosebumps had gone now, and her skin was warm to the touch, and softer than he could ever imagine. He kissed her neck and shoulders then tore away what little remained of her clothing and slowly, intently, explored every inch of her nakedness. The goosebumps returned as Aaron's hands and mouth caressed Katya's lively, willing body like a thousand silk handkerchiefs, intensifying her already fiercely burning desire.

"I want you to make love to me," she whispered breathlessly into his ear.

He looked into her eyes, and then kissed her passionately on the lips, draining the last of her remaining strength.

"You will be my first," she said with a slight nervousness in her voice.

Aaron touched a finger to her lips. "You are mine as well," he said quietly. "You can trust me, Katya. I will honor you." He kissed her lips again, gently this time. She closed her eyes as in a dream.

Then, as the sun slowly settled into the Pacific, he patiently and carefully made himself one with her.

Cabo San Lucas, Mexico

Chapter 39

James Harness and Larry Holt took a taxi from southern Baja's *Aeródromo Internacional* into downtown Cabo San Lucas, Mexico. It was hot outside. Really hot. After questioning several locals, the two ended up at the infamous Cabo Wabo Cantina.

The nightclub was huge, with a stage and a set of drums toward the back, and wild, festive lighting and decorations covering every inch of the space. However, considering it wasn't even 6:00 p.m. yet, the men weren't surprised to see that it was deserted.

As they approached the bar, Harness pointed out a wall full of Van Halen memorabilia, and Holt was first to notice the vast collection of ladies underwear hanging above their heads.

It was hotter in the Cantina than it was outside, and Officer Holt looked at Harness expectantly. Harness looked back at him with a look that said, *What the hell do you want?*

"Are you gonna buy your partner a drink or do I have to buy it myself?" Holt said. "And don't feed me any of your bullshit about us being on duty. If I can't have a drink in fucking Cabo San ... Wabo, where the hell *can* I drink?"

Harness gave him a disgusted look. "I'm a little busy at the moment," he said, jerking his head toward the bartender to remind Holt that they were there to gather information, not to get drunk. "And if we *were* on duty, I'd have your badge for insubordination and abusive language."

"Fuck you," Holt said.

Harness turned to the bartender. "Two shots of your best tequila and two beer backs, please."

"I'd buy my own damn drink if you'd pay me once in a while," Holt mumbled.

"Whatever makes the big baby happy," Harness said.

"Kiss my big black ass," Holt said.

They watched with dry throats as the bartender poured the shots and delivered their order to the bar.

Holt threw back his shot and chased it with his entire beer. He hoped that everything he'd heard about the potency of Cabo Wabo's tequila was true, since it was unlikely he could pry another dollar out of Harness's wallet.

"You're not supposed to chug the beer, Holt," Harness said. "It's for sipping."

"Where'd you come up with *that?*" Holt said. "And why don't you just shut up about it?"

Harness downed his shot as well, along with a sip of beer, and then he introduced himself and showed the bartender Jason's picture, offering him the usual $50 cash incentive.

"He looks a lot different out of uniform," the bartender said, stuffing the $50 in his tip jar. "But yeah, I saw him. About three days ago. He was with a hot redhead and some young guy that looked like a surfer or something. They had dinner and drinks ... lots of drinks."

"Three days ago, did you say?"

"Yeah, Tuesday night, I think," the bartender said. "I heard them say something about San Diego."

"Did they say anything else?" Harness asked.

"I don't know ... They were all pretty hammered by then."

Harness shoved another $50 across the bar.

The bartender scooped up the bill and glanced around the empty club, and then he leaned toward Harness, as if he were going to divulge a national secret. Holt leaned in as well.

"Here's where it started getting really weird," the bartender said in a near whisper. "The guy you're looking for? The guy in the picture? He started going off about a plot to assassinate some high-level official in the United States government."

"What?" Harness said. "He had to be bullshitting."

"How the hell should I know?" the bartender said. "But he was talking about *torpedoing* the son-of-a-bitch."

"Yeah, right," Holt said. "Where's the guy gonna get a torpedo? Fucking Walmart?"

"He mentioned an old Russian submarine that's part of some museum in San Diego," the bartender said.

"*Cobra*," Harness said to Holt. "She's moored at the MMSD. But she barely *floats*." But he knew better than to underestimate his adversary's resourcefulness.

"Just telling you what I heard," the bartender said.

"His companions," Harness said. "Were they in on it?"

"It was hard to tell ... they were pretty fucked up. But I doubt it. It was a one-sided conversation at that point, and the guy didn't seem to care if they were listening or not."

"The redhead," Harness said. "What did she look like?"

"She was hot," the bartender said.

"That's it? A hundred bucks and I get 'She was hot'?"

"What do you want from me?" the bartender said, annoyed now. "Beautiful face, long, flaming red hair, smokin' body ... You're the *detective* ... *You* describe her."

"Okay, okay, I get it. She's hot," Harness said. "No need to get your panties in a bunch. Did they say anything about a day and time? For the assassination, I mean."

The Bartender paused for a moment. "Friday night, I think."

Harness turned to Holt. "What day is today?"

"How the fuck should I know?" Holt said.

"Today *is* Friday, come to think of it," the bartender said.

"Damn it!" Harness said. "How long does it take to get from here to San Diego on a motor-yacht?"

"San Diego? Under power? Oh, I'd say two or three days tops — assuming the weather holds, and including stopping for fuel."

Harness checked his watch and looked at Holt. "It's 6:00 p.m. If they left here Tuesday, they could be there by now."

He turned back to the bartender. "How long's a flight from here to San Diego?"

"Two hours and ten minutes."

Harness thought maybe he could get a call off to Naval Command in Point Loma. "Do cell phones work here?" he asked.

"Not necessarily. You'd have to arrange that with your provider, and the dialing out is different here. And you need to understand basic Spanish because the operator recordings are —"

"Do you have a house phone?" Harness demanded.

"Yes, but it'll only handle local calls," the bartender said.

Harness couldn't believe his luck. Here he was, stuck down in Cabo San Lucas while Jason Souther attempted to bring America to its knees. He asked the bartender to call a taxi.

"Drink up, Holt," he said, sliding his nearly full glass of beer in his direction. "I think our problems just got a lot more serious."

NAVAL BASE POINT LOMA
SAN DIEGO

Chapter 40

The Executive Officer checked his watch. 7:00 p.m. The final security arrangements had been made, and now he had the privilege of escorting the President of the United States and his four secret servicemen on board the 362-foot nuclear submarine USS *Hampton*, joining its standard complement of 12 officers and 98 crewmen. He unhooked the maroon-velvet rope guarding the gangway.

"Are you ready, sir?" he asked.

"It's that time already?" the President said.

"You seem nervous, sir," the XO said.

The President *was* a bit apprehensive about riding along on the Emergency Nighttime Surface Drill, but he wasn't sure why. "Just some pre-cruise jitters, is all," he said.

"There's no reason to worry, Mr. President," the XO said. "Tonight's is just a routine drill on board a technological marvel, commanded by one of the finest officers in the Navy."

The agent with the carnation gave him a look that said, *You better not be bullshitting, asshole ...*

"If you would follow me, gentlemen?" the XO said, and they proceeded up the gangway.

The captain of the submarine, Commander Adam Byrd, greeted the President on the bridge. "Welcome aboard, sir," he said.

"Thank you, Commander," the President said, shaking his hand. "I hear I'm in for quite a treat tonight."

"That you are," Commander Byrd said.

An ensign walked over holding a small bundle of nylon webbing. "The ride may be a little rough, Mr. President," he said. "This is a safety harness for you to wear. I'll let you know when it's time to hook up."

This didn't exactly fill the President with confidence, but he did as requested and stepped into the rig.

The agent with the flower looked at the ensign indignantly, wondering why he and his Secret Service team didn't rate safety gear of their own.

THE PARTY

San Diego Waterfront

Chapter 41

Uri Ruden was first to arrive at the party. It had started to rain, and the framework holding the stretched plastic structure covering b-39 strained against an increasingly strong wind.

He ducked through the opening in the plastic and crossed the temporary wooden gangplank onto the submarine's deck then he powered up a couple of the construction crew's work lights to illuminate the area for the benefit of the other guests.

Uri was pleased to see that all of the safety handrails, walkways, ramps, and stairs that the museum had installed for visitors had been removed, and the holes repaired. He would perform a hull-pressure test later to confirm that the welds met his specifications.

He entered the submarine through the fin hatch and climbed down the ladder to the Control Room. It was from there in Compartment Three that they would be piloting the submarine. He went over the procedures in his mind and re-familiarized himself with the helm controls, and then he headed to the Forward Torpedo Room.

Uri Ruden inspected the torpedoes. The red and white one was on the rack, and the green one was still loaded into tube 5.

He reviewed the launch procedure in his mind. The shot would be at close range, so they would not be using the fire-control system. They would simply aim the sub straight at the target using the attack periscope, and fire the torpedo from the bow tube, hoping for the best.

Satisfied that everything was in order, he closed tube 5's inner hatch cover and returned to the Control Room.

Next to arrive were Jason and Brandy. They met Uri Ruden in the Control Room, and Jason introduced him to Brandy.

"If I'd known there would be beautiful women at the party I would have dressed up a little," Uri said.

Brandy noticed that Uri was in full dress uniform and she smiled. They shook hands and exchanged pleasantries.

"Why don't we head down to the galley and make ourselves some drinks?" Uri said.

Brandy had no problem with that. She could use a stiff drink about now.

"Sounds good," Jason said, and they ducked through the watertight hatch leading to Compartment Four.

Jason and Uri were too tall to stand comfortably in the tiny galley, so Brandy had the honor of mixing the drinks. When she was ready she joined them in the corridor and they touched paper cups, toasting nothing in particular.

Uri looked at his watch and said, "Will you excuse us, Brandy? I have something to discuss with Jason. If you need us, we'll be two doors down, there in the Midshipmen's Cabin, just beyond the pantry."

"No problem," Brandy said. "I'll catch up with you later."

The men turned and walked down the corridor.

"Pour me another Scotch, will you, Brandy?" Jason said over his shoulder. "We'll only be a minute."

He followed Uri into the Midshipmen's Cabin and closed the door.

Left with nothing to do, Brandy downed her drink, mixed two more, and then headed down the corridor toward the Engine Room to explore the rest of the sub.

Chapter 42

A light rain continued to fall as Aaron dropped Katya off at the dock. She kissed him and then ran inside the gift shop to change. Aaron motored across to the *Cayman Jewel* to do the same.

They met back at the dock a few minutes later.

"You look amazing," Aaron said, at the sight of Katya's dress.

Katya beamed. "You don't look so bad yourself." She had never seen him in long pants before. She kissed him hard on the lips, and then hand in hand they walked down to the submarine.

Through the rain they saw that the big plastic tarpaulin had already been completed and that it covered the entire sub. The gangway was gone, replaced by a simple temporary wooden gangplank that led through a narrow opening in the tarp.

"I wonder why they had to do *that?*" Aaron said as they ducked inside.

All of the tourist handrails and walkways were missing. And as they walked up on deck they saw that the bow and stern stairways leading down into the submarine were gone as well, and the openings welded shut.

Aaron figured it was all part of the restoration project and decided not to dwell on it.

They entered the submarine through the fin hatch and climbed down the ladder to an empty Control Room.

Just as she stepped off the ladder, Katya remembered that she had forgotten to lock up the gift shop.

"I'm such a space head," she said. "I think I forgot to lock up."

"Two days on the job and you're the one who locks up?"

She held the key up like a trophy. "My father had to pull some strings to get me this job, and I don't want to screw it up."

"While you're gone I think I'll check out the Captain's Cabin. Can you find your own way out?"

"Of course, silly," Katya said. "I'm not *incompetent*."

Aaron laughed. "Go on then," he said. "I'll be in Compartment Two, right through there." He pointed to one of the two watertight hatches leading out of the Control Room, the one near the helm controls. "Last door on the left, I think. You can't miss it."

"I'll find it," Katya said. "Back in a flash." She gave him a peck on the cheek and then climbed back up the ladder exiting the submarine.

The Captain's Cabin was a tiny room, the width of the bunk against the back wall, with a small writing desk on the left. The Maritime Museum had outfitted the room with period pieces for the benefit of the tourists: a Soviet Captain's jacket, some playing cards, and an old, framed photograph of Leonid Brezhnev, General Secretary of the

Central Committee of the Communist Party of the Soviet Union.

Some of the playing cards had spilled on the floor, and Aaron considered picking them up; then he figured the museum had placed them there to add authenticity, so he left them alone.

Katya returned from the gift shop and made her way back down the ladder to the Control Room.

She ducked through the hatch leading to Compartment Two, looking for the Captain's Cabin, but there *was* no Captain's Cabin ...

In her confusion, Katya had gotten completely turned around, and instead of Compartment Two, she was in Compartment Four, and she had run out of cabins. The only room left in the compartment was the galley, and beyond that a dark space that led to the Engine Room.

She tried calling Aaron on her cell phone, but there was no service, so she turned and headed back down the corridor toward the Control Room.

When she came to the door with the small sign that read MIDSHIPMEN'S CABIN, she stopped, thinking maybe Aaron had gotten the cabin name wrong. But as she went to knock, she overheard two men talking inside — and neither of them sounded like Aaron.

Either he's being really quiet, or he's not in there, she thought. Then she held her head up to the door and listened ...

"I met with Commander Fagan and Captain Zaane today," Jason said. "The President's VIP cruise is all set. The USS *Hampton* will head out at 9:00 p.m. tonight as scheduled. The *Neau Islander* will depart the dock at 8:15, and hit the main channel by 8:30. By 8:35 Cobra should be beneath her wake as she escorts us to Ballast Point before heading out to sea."

"That's great news," Uri said. "We should be hiding under the bait barges no later than 8:55."

"Fagan told me you were in charge of Cobra's weaponry," Jason said. "Can you tell me what type of bomb we're packing?"

"I've armed Cobra with a conventional, high-explosive torpedo with enough fire power to cut the *Hampton* in half," Uri said. "The President will never know what hit him."

Katya clutched the front of her dress. *Oh my God,* she thought. She had heard rumors of a Presidential visit to San Diego, but this plot to assassinate him sounded too absurd to be true.

"I wish we could nuke the bastards," Jason said. "Just to be sure. But I suppose the collateral damage would be unacceptable — not to mention suicidal."

"You're right," Uri said. "It would be suicidal."

Katya suddenly felt an urgent need to find Aaron. She headed back to the Control Room to try again.

Chapter 43

Katya managed to find her way back to the Control Room, but as she looked around at the confusing array of hardware, she feared that she may still be lost.

Just then a woman with long red hair appeared in the hatch Katya had just come through. The woman was clutching a paper cup in each hand, spilling most of their contents while ducking through the low opening.

"Oh, hi," the woman said, seeing Katya. "Who are you?"

"Uh — my name is Ekatarina," Katya said, a little off guard. The woman was *very* pretty. "Who are you?"

"I'm Brandy," she said, glancing down at her alcohol soaked fingers. "I'd shake your hand, but —"

"That's okay," Katya said quickly. "I was looking for my date. His name is Aaron and I really need to find him."

"Aaron Quinn?" Brandy said, surprised.

"You know him?" Katya said.

"We've met," Brandy said curtly, still harboring a grudge for what happened in Panama. "But I haven't seen him." She gave Katya a quick look up and down, as if to determine whether or not she was worthy of him.

"I'm here with Jason Beckham," she boasted, as if he were a famous celebrity. "He's currently in a meeting, but I expect him back soon."

"You'll have to excuse me, Brandy, but I —"

"*Looking for me?*" a man's voice said from behind.

Katya whirled around and swallowed hard, certain she was facing one of the men plotting the assassination.

"Oh, hi, Jason," Brandy said. "We were just talking about you." She handed him the remains of one of the paper-cup cocktails and gestured toward Katya. "This is Ekatarina. She's looking for Aaron."

Jason was struck by Katya's rare beauty. "Jason Beckham," he said, offering her his hand. "You must be Captain Pankov's daughter."

Katya hesitated, and then shook Jason's hand quickly, as if he were a leper. There was no doubt he was one of them. *I can't believe I'm touching one of the men plotting to kill the President of the United States!* She shuddered and glanced around for a good place to throw up.

Jason was accustomed to women being uncomfortable in his presence, and normally it was due to his irresistible charm and powerful, animal magnetism. However, Ekatarina clearly found him repulsive, and this was new to him, and he didn't appreciate it.

Suddenly Katya spotted the hatch near the helm controls, and kicked herself, thinking, *That's that hatch leading to the Captain's Cabin, you idiot! Not the other one!* If only she hadn't blundered into Compartment Four. Life would have been a whole lot simpler!

She looked at Jason and Brandy and forced herself to be polite. "I-it was nice meeting you," she said. "But if you will excuse me, I have to go find my date. Maybe we'll see you at the party."

"What party?" Brandy said sarcastically, gesturing to the vacant space surrounding them.

Katya laughed nervously then waved a quick goodbye and ducked through the hatch in search of Aaron.

Jason was shocked to hear that Aaron was Ekatarina's date. The very idea of a punk like him being with a woman of her caliber, a woman he would clearly never have, turned him to stone. He made a mental note to rectify the situation as soon as the opportunity presented itself.

Chapter 44

Finally, Katya was in Compartment Two. She made her way down the corridor to the Captain's Cabin and was relieved to see that the door was open. She peeked inside and saw Aaron seated on the bunk reading something tacked to the wall. At his feet were a few playing cards, scattered randomly about.

She tapped on the doorframe.

"Oh — hi, Katya," Aaron said. "I was beginning to think you weren't coming back. Did you get everything locked up?"

"I need to talk to you," Katya whispered quickly.

Aaron stood up from the bunk. "Is everything all right?"

"I'm not sure," Katya said, gesturing for him to keep his voice down. She glanced down the corridor toward the Control Room where she'd left Jason and Brandy.

"Come in and shut the door," Aaron said.

"Somewhere more private," Katya said.

Aaron could tell by the look in Katya's eyes that she had something very serious to tell him. He thought of the Forward Torpedo Room next door. It was tucked deep into the bow of the boat, and he doubted there was anywhere more private.

"Follow me," he said.

He took her hand and led her through the watertight hatch leading next door to Compartment One. He swung the hatch cover shut and cranked the locking handle tight.

Katya's brain hurt. She pressed her fingers to her temples and took a moment to collect herself. "I got lost, and I ended up in the wrong end of this *stupid* submarine. So I was heading back and I overheard two men talking in the Midshipman's Cabin, with door closed ... a-and I swear on my mother's grave, Aaron, they were talking about a plot to kill the President of the United States."

"*What?*"

She knew how ridiculous it sounded, but she had to get it out. "The President is here in San Diego, and he's going on a VIP cruise on a nuclear submarine ... and these men are planning to torpedo it."

"That's the craziest thing I've —"

"Why would I feed you a bunch of *lies*, Aaron? I heard them! This is *for real!*" Tears welled in her eyes.

An icy chill ran down Aaron's spine as suddenly he recalled that crazy night when he, Jason, and Brandy got drunk together in that nightclub down in Cabo San Lucas. He had assumed that all of the memories of that night had been lost to a severe tequila hangover. But he'd been wrong.

"Did they say when they're planning to do this?" he said firmly.

"I-I don't know," Katya said. "I left before they —."

"Did you see their faces?"

"No. The door was closed. But I'm positive one of the men was Jason Beckham."

Aaron ran his hand through his hair. How could this be? *Katya's wild story was the same story Jason himself had told him and Brandy that night in the Cabo Wabo Cantina!*

"We have to tell someone," he said. "We have to let someone know, and *quickly.*"

He checked his cell phone, but there was no service. "Wait here," he said. "I need to see if we can get off this boat without attracting attention."

Katya looked at him doubtfully. "What if someone decides to load a torpedo or something?"

"You're right," he said.

He took Katya's hand and led her out of the Forward Torpedo Room and back into the Captain's Cabin.

Katya sat on the small bunk, looking up at Aaron with fear in her eyes.

"Keep the door locked until I return," Aaron said. "I won't be long."

"Hurry, okay?"

"Like the wind," he said then stepped out and closed the door behind him.

Jason had sent Brandy to the galley for fresh cocktails and had followed Katya into Compartment Two.

He hid in the Ward Room and waited until she and Aaron came out of the Forward Torpedo Room, and then, as soon as Aaron left, he stepped out and walked slowly down the narrow corridor toward the Captain's Cabin.

Chapter 45

Katya waited alone on the bunk in the Captain's Cabin, nervously pushing one of the playing cards around with her toe. She heard a click, and saw the door handle slowly turn, but instinctively she knew it wasn't Aaron, and her heart leaped up into her throat.

She had forgotten to lock it!

She jumped up and tried to shut the door, but the man jammed it with his foot, peering in at her with one eye through the narrow opening.

It was *Jason*.

"Hello, Katya," he said calmly. "May I come in?"

"W-what are you doing here?" Katya said. "The party's somewhere else."

"I'm here to remind you that Aaron is just a boy," he said, "and that what you really need is a man."

Katya found that unbearably insulting on many levels. Aaron Quinn was *definitely* not a boy. But she knew it would be best to be friendly and try to calmly discourage Jason. *Keep it cool, Katya. For the love of God, keep it cool.*

"You're right," she said, struggling to hide the tremble in her voice. "I like real men *way* more than boys. But we can't be fooling around here on this silly submarine, can we? Someone might see us. Why don't we meet somewhere more private?" It sounded fake and patronizing and Katya knew she hadn't done herself any favors.

Jason agreed.

He forced his way in and grabbed her left arm, spinning her around with her back to him, holding her close to his chest. She tried to pull away, but he tightened his grip, cupping his free hand firmly over her right breast.

"Why are you fighting me?" he said, teeth clenched. "You know you want it."

Jason had a death grip on her arm. "Please," she said. "You're hurting me ... Please don't do this."

Jason's hand moved from her breast and slid down between her legs. The hot breath on her neck that would normally have turned her on only made her nauseous. *Oh, my God,* she thought. *This can't be happening. Do something Katya. Don't give in to him. THINK girl. THINK!*

She steeled herself and decided to give the asshole one last thing to consider. "I'll scream, Jason," she said. "This cabin door is thin, and I swear to God if you do this I'll scream so fucking loud your eardrums will bleed and this entire submarine will split in two and sink to the bottom of San Diego *fucking* Bay."

Jason smiled and flipped open the blade of a long, very sharp knife, holding it flat against her cheekbone. "You do and I'll kill you," he said calmly. "Right here — right now. Is that really what you want?"

If that's what it will take to make you stop, Katya thought, *then yes! That's exactly what I want!*

Brandy Fine had entered Compartment Two looking for Jason. She had already downed the last two cocktails she had made and had a fresh one in each hand. She was feeling the alcohol and was anxious to get the party started.

She walked down the narrow corridor checking each room, and when she neared the Captain's Cabin she heard a scream.

She threw the drinks to one side and tried the door, and to her surprise it opened, and what she saw inside tore through her heart like flying shrapnel: Jason Beckham was sprawled across a struggling, terrified girl named Ekatarina.

"*HEY!*" Brandy shouted. "*What the hell are you DOING?*"

Jason started, easing his hold on Katya, and then he stood and folded his knife into his pocket. Katya jumped up and ran to Brandy, tears flowing down her face.

"You lousy son-of-a-bitch," Brandy said, holding Katya tightly in her arms. She wanted to tear Jason's lungs out and feed them to him with a fork.

Jason just stood there looking smug.

Brandy straightened Katy's dress and took her by the hand. "Come, sweetie," she said. "Let's get you far away from this psychotic *sicko*."

She led Katya out of the Captain's Cabin and headed for the nearest watertight hatch: Compartment One, the Forward Torpedo Room.

Brandy swung the heavy hatch cover closed, and then turned to Katya, taking her gently by the shoulders. "Let me look at you," she said, looking her up and down. "Did he hurt you? What did he do to you?"

Katya was trembling, tears and mascara streaming down her cheeks. Brandy could see that an angry bruise was forming on her upper arm. She gave Katya a gentle, swaying hug. Katya hugged her back gratefully.

"H-he had a knife," Katya said, sobbing. "He said he would —"

"Damn him!" Brandy cried. "I'll *kill* that fucking asshole." She picked up a heavy piece of iron pipe. "If Jason Beckham is stupid enough to show his ugly face in here, I'll crack his *fucking* skull."

Chapter 46

Just then Richard Fagan drove up and parked along the boardwalk near the Maritime Museum. His girlfriend, Martha, was in the car with him.

"You go on ahead," he said to her. "I'll meet you on the sub. I have to make a quick call."

Martha did as she was told.

Fagan took out his phone and called Captain Henk Zaane, giving him the scheduled departure time for the President's VIP tour.

"So we're good to go?" Fagan asked.

"Affirmative," Captain Zaane said. He would adjust *Neau Islander's* departure time accordingly. "I'll churn up some good foam for you."

Fagan smiled. "You do that, Captain," he said. "We can use all the cover we can get."

He hung up and went to find Martha.

Chapter 47

"You sit here and rest," Brandy said, helping Katya to a seat in a corner. "Where the hell's Aaron? Did you ever find him?"

Katya wiped the tears from her face with the backs of her fingers and then relayed everything she'd overheard about the plot to assassinate the President, telling Brandy that Jason Beckham was involved.

Brandy was speechless. Then, just as Aaron had done, she recalled the wild story Jason had told them that night down in Mexico in the Cabo Wabo Cantina.

Oh my dear God, she thought. *That load of drunken crap Jason fed me and Aaron that night in Cabo was TRUE! Why did we not SEE that?*

"Aaron went to see if there's a safe way for us to get off the submarine," Katya said. "So he'll be looking for me. But he thinks I'm in the Captain's Cabin."

"I'll watch for him," Brandy said. She adjusted her grip on her iron-pipe club, and pulled the hatch cover open a little, leaving it slightly ajar.

"How are you feeling?" Brandy asked. "How's your arm?"

"I guess I'm okay," Katya said, finding that her new bruise was tender to the touch. "I just wish Aaron would come back so we can get off this god-forsaken *submarine*."

"You and me both," Brandy said.

"How long have you known him?" Katya asked.

"Aaron? Oh, just a few weeks," Brandy said. "We sailed up here to San Diego from the Caymans together, so I got to know him pretty well."

"Would you want him? If you weren't already with Jason, that is?"

Brandy looked at her, surprised. "You mean as a boyfriend?"

"Yes, Brandy," Katya said. "As a boyfriend."

Brandy smiled to herself. Ekatarina was so young and naive. She could never understand what she and Aaron had been through together, and how close they really were.

She wanted to tell her about how whenever Jason was busy at the helm, they would sit together, just the two of them, talking for hours under a brilliant canopy of Caribbean stars.

She wanted to tell her about how Aaron had looked at her with desire in his eyes that morning on the Panama Canal, and how close they had come to making love.

But what good would it do to go on about what might have been? Aaron was Ekatarina's man now.

"Yes, my dear," she said at last. "Yes, I would want him."

"I'm hoping to marry Aaron one day," Katya said.

Brandy sighed. She could only dream of doing that. For better or for worse, she was with Jason, and she had a wedding ring to prove it.

Chapter 48

Uri Ruden was up on deck checking out something near the stern of the boat. He saw Aaron and acknowledged him. Aaron walked over and said hello, acting as if nothing was wrong.

"Just taking a look at some of the repairs," Uri said. "This used to be the emergency escape hatch. Not much good now, though, since they welded it shut. Wouldn't want to try and escape from *this* sub."

Aaron thought about that for a moment.

"How's the party going?" Uri asked.

"To be honest, it's kinda not," Aaron said.

"Commander Fagan should be here soon," Uri said. "He'll get things rolling."

"Are you expecting anyone else?" Aaron asked.

"Fagan will bring his girlfriend, Martha, of course," Uri said, "and Captain Pankov is flying in from Russia ... but I'm not sure if he'll show tonight."

Katya's father's coming? Aaron thought. It was appearing more and more unlikely that he and Katya could slip away from the party unnoticed.

"What do you say we go below and wait for them?" Uri said. "I'm ready for another drink."

"You go on ahead," Aaron said. "I'll be along in a minute."

Uri nodded and went below.

Aaron tried his cell phone, but there was still no service.

He was about to go below again to find Katya when he heard what sounded like a pair of high heels crossing the wooden gangplank. He stepped behind the fin, and when the woman stepped through the opening in the tarp he saw that she was alone.

He froze. The woman looked familiar. *Oh, my God,* he thought.

He blinked hard and looked again. *Could it be?* Her hair was different, and she was very thin, but it was definitely her. It was Aaron's *mother! Ashley Quinn!*

He wanted to leap for joy and yell, *Mom! It's me. Aaron! You're alive! Oh my God! You're alive!*

But as he stepped out from behind the fin preparing to give her a huge hug, all she did was stop and look at him.

"May I help you?" she said.

For a moment Aaron could only stand there staring. His mother had never looked at him that way before. It was as if she were looking at a total stranger.

"Y-you don't remember me, do you," he said at last.

"No ..." she said, looking at him expectantly. "Should I?"

Is it because I'm older? Aaron thought. *Or has something terrible happened to her because of the accident? Certainly she would recognize her own son — no matter how long it's been. Has she lost her memory?*

"I'm sorry," he said. "For a moment I thought I knew you. My name is Aaron."

"I'm Martha," she said, relaxing a bit now.

Martha? What happened to Ashley? His mother *had* lost her memory.

He noticed she'd been crying, and his urge to hug her, to comfort her, grew even stronger. But he refrained.

"Would you like for me to show you the way to the party?" he said. "Submarines can be very intimidating."

Ashley looked back in the direction of the dock. "That's very kind of you Aaron, but actually I'm waiting for someone."

He could tell that she was extremely upset. Something had frightened her — and not that long ago. He wanted to take her away from there, but he knew that she would never leave with him — not yet, at least. He would have to figure out a way to get both Katya *and* his mother off the sub.

"Perhaps we'll talk later," he said. "It was nice meeting you, Martha."

And with a little wave, he went below to find Katya.

Chapter 49

Aaron climbed down the ladder to the Control Room and then ducked through the hatch into Compartment Two, making his way to the Captain's Cabin. But when he got there the door was open and Katya was gone.

Damn it, he thought. *I should never have left her alone.*

Panic tugged at his heart as he turned to head back to the Control Room.

"*Pssst*," a voice whispered from behind him.

He jumped, and then turned to see Brandy Fine waving to him from inside the hatch leading to the Forward Torpedo Room.

"*Brandy?*" he said. "What are you —"

"*Shhh*," she said, gesturing for him to come. "*In here — I have Ekatarina.*"

Chapter 50

Jason had pulled himself together and returned to the Control Room. He would deal with the girls later.

Uri Ruden had just stepped off the ladder from the deck.

"Where's Fagan?" Jason said to him.

"Oh, hi, Jason," Uri said. "I haven't seen him yet."

Just then Fagan and his girlfriend came down the ladder. Jason did a double-take: it was the woman from the photo on Fagan's mantel — and she was even more breathtaking in person.

Fagan straightened his naval officer's dress uniform and shook Jason's and Uri's hands. "This is Martha," he said, indicating Ashley. "Martha, I'd like you to meet my friends ... Uri Ruden and Jason Souther."

Ashley went cold. *So you're the infamous Jason Souther,* she thought. His features looked unsettlingly familiar but she couldn't recall why.

Jason was totally enamored of her.

Uri offered Ashley his hand, which she shook with a polite nod.

Jason held out his hand as well. "It's pleasure to meet you," he said.

But Ashley only stared back at him, her throat dry. There was no doubt in her mind that there was some sort of connection between him and her forgotten past, and it wasn't good.

Fagan was focused on the mission. "I'm glad you're both here," he said to the men. "I'd like to meet for a few minutes before the party gets underway."

Uri turned to Ashley. "Martha, if you wish, there are drinks in the galley." He pointed in the direction of Compartment Four and repeated the familiar instructions: "Through that hatch and down the corridor on the right."

He turned to the men. "I'll meet you gentlemen in the officer's Ward Room in five minutes," he said, and then headed to the Forward Torpedo Room.

Fagan and Jason stepped into the Ward Room and closed the door.

Ashley looked around the cramped Control Room, feeling utterly alone. The combination of the suffocating closeness and an anatomical maze of pipes and wires made her feel as if she'd been swallowed by some sort of bionic whale.

She looked back on her meeting with Aaron up on deck and wondered why he had made such an impression on her. It was like she had known him for years ... or maybe her whole life.

Her head hurt and she thought of trying to find the galley and mix herself a drink. But she hadn't heard a word of Uri's directions and the sub's dim, cluttered interior *was* intimidating. Not knowing what else to do, she took a seat at the chart table and waited.

Chapter 51

"Aaron!" Katya cried, giving him a big hug as he stepped through the hatch. "I'm so glad you're all right. I was beginning to *worry*."

Aaron saw that she'd been crying, and then he noticed the bruise. "What has *happened* to you?" he said.

Brandy glanced at Katya. "She asked me not to tell you this, Aaron, but Jason just tried to rape her."

"Oh, my God," Aaron said. He thought he knew Jason pretty well. "Are you certain?"

"I think I'd *know* when I'm about to be raped, *Aaron*," Katya said, her eyes filling with tears again.

He looked at her, feeling stupid. "You're right. I am so sorry. Of course you would know."

Brandy gave him a look that said, *Good one, you idiot*. "Ekatarina told me about the plot to kill the President," she said.

"So you know," Aaron said.

"I do," Brandy said. "But I'm having trouble comprehending it."

"There's one other complication," Aaron said.

The girls looked at him expectantly — as if they didn't have enough to worry about.

"My Mom's here," Aaron said.

"*What?*" Katya said.

Brandy was unsure as to the real significance of this news, but she could tell that it hovered somewhere between really good and really bad.

Katya was incredulous. "But you said your mother was killed in the —"

"I know, Katya. That's what I thought. Hell, that's what the police put it in their damn *report*. They must have skipped the forensics investigation altogether and hauled the damn Aston Martin straight to the freakin' scrap yard!" He paused. "All I know is she's alive ... and she's on this damn submarine with us."

Just then footsteps could be heard coming their way.

"Over here," Aaron whispered. "Quickly."

Aaron helped Katya and Brandy tuck in with him in the small, dark space behind the starboard torpedo rack, just as someone stepped in through the watertight hatch.

It was Uri Ruden.

The three held their breath.

Uri opened torpedo tube 5's inner hatch cover and saw that the green torpedo was still loaded and ready. He jumped, when out of nowhere Commander Fagan stepped through the hatch.

"Oh, hello, Commander," Uri said. "May I help you?"

"I thought I'd stop in and check out our torpedo," Fagan said.

"Oh — yes, of course," Uri said. "But I was just leaving to go to our meeting."

"I'll just be a minute," Fagan said.

He checked the red torpedo hanging on the starboard torpedo rack, but could tell by its markings that it was the dummy. Then he saw a green torpedo loaded in tube 5 and walked over to take a look.

Uri knew that in a few seconds Fagan was going to be very unhappy. "We really should get to our meeting. The party has already started."

"In a second," Fagan said. He noticed the unusual shape of the tail and the guidance fins, and the special electronics connector. He checked the torpedo's markings: *VA-111 Shkval.*

"Hold on just a second," Fagan said, the hair on his neck standing up. "This is a damn *Shkval.* A supercavitating rocket propelled bomb. It's a freakin' *nuke*, Uri!"

Aaron and the girls couldn't believe their ears. Things had just gone from terrible to horrifying.

"You are correct," Uri said calmly, figuring the cat was out of the bag anyway. "The *VA-111 Shkval.* A solid-rocket propelled torpedo achieving a high velocity of 230 mph by producing an envelope of supercavitating bubbles which coat the entire weapon surface in a thin layer of gas, causing the metal skin of the weapon to avoid contact with the water, significantly reducing drag, and —."

"Cut the crap, Uri. I know how the damn thing works. Nobody said anything about using a nuke! How did you get this?"

"From our guy in Seattle, of course," Uri said.

"Okay, but you and I agreed to have him load one dummy torpedo and one conventional explosive."

"Yes, and I told him to replace the conventional weapon with a nuclear warhead," Uri said frankly.

"Why the *fuck* would you do that?" Fagan said. "And where the *hell* did he come up with a *Shkval?* Talk about *rare.* Not to mention that fact that it'll probably explode before it exits the damn *tube*." He slammed tube 5's inner hatch cover closed. "The deal's *off*, Ruden. You hear me? It's *off!* I didn't sign on for a damn *suicide mission!"*

Suddenly from behind him a voice said, "I'm sorry you feel that way, Commander."

Fagan whirled around to see the face of Vtorak Borisovich Pankov sighting down the barrel of his .45 caliber pistol at very close range.

"*Pankov!*" Fagan exclaimed. "You made it! Uh — Uri and I were just checking out our torpedo."

Aaron snuck a glance at Katya that said, *Your father's in on this?* But she could only wish with all her heart it wasn't true.

"The nuclear warhead was my idea," Pankov said.

"But why? Fagan said. "What could you possibly hope to —"

"You know as well as I do, Commander," Pankov said, interrupting him, "mission failure is not an option. We can't take a chance on merely *damaging* the President's sub. We must *destroy it*."

"But we *can't miss*, Captain," Fagan argued. "We'll be right on top of them. *How can we miss?*"

Uri Ruden stepped up to add his two cents. "Why squander a chance to take out one third of the United States's entire Naval Pacific Fleet, as well as downtown San Diego's financial district?"

Fagan looked at the two men and his heart fell. He knew it was futile to argue. He decided to take a different tack. "If you do this, Captain," he said, "the explosion will take *us* out too, you know. You, Uri here, and Jason Souther."

"I am aware of that, Commander," Pankov said calmly. "But you said yourself you would do anything to see this mission succeed."

"You're right," Fagan said. "I *do* want the President dead. And I'd be willing to sacrifice myself and a few good Navy men to make it happen. But not an entire *city!* or the *entire world!*"

"Let's say we did use a conventional weapon," Uri said, "and we were lucky enough to survive the blast. Just how did you figure we would get away, Commander? Where would you have had us go?"

"I figured in the attending confusion it would work itself out," Fagan said quickly. "But it's not my life I'm concerned about ... it's those of millions of innocent civilians."

He turned to Pankov. "Please reconsider, Captain. As one officer to another ... I'm begging you. *Please* stop this madness. We're looking at starting World War III here."

Pankov leveled his gun on Fagan. "Goodbye, Commander," said. "We appreciate your service to your country."

"Father, *NO!*" Katya screamed.

Aaron reached to cover her mouth, but he was too late.

Fagan saw his chance and dove for Pankov's gun. The girls screamed as the two men crashed into the torpedo rack and fought wildly, flying from one side of the small chamber to the other, exchanging punches, kicking, and clawing each other in a desperate, chaotic fight.

Uri cowered up against a set of valves, the girls screaming and crying, the men smashing each other's faces, spattering blood around the room. Aaron danced back and forth, searching for an opening through which he could help

Fagan — but all he had was his pocketknife, and the struggle was much too violent.

At last Fagan managed to knock Pankov's gun free and haul him to the floor where he raised his fist to deliver a knockout blow.

Pop!

The silenced bullet entered Fagan's back through his ribcage, piercing his heart. He went limp and rolled onto the floor, dead.

Pankov turned to see Jason Souther standing next to the watertight hatch, a thin stream of smoke curling out his pistol barrel.

"Having a little problem, Captain?" Jason said. He had heard everything.

Pankov got to his feet and straightened his rumpled uniform. He was covered in blood, his hair flying wildly about his head, the cuts on his face and lips purple and bleeding.

"It is dangerous to discharge a weapon aboard a submarine, Jason," he said calmly, spitting blood.

"Duly noted, sir," Jason said.

Pankov found a rag and wiped most of the blood from his face, and then he picked up his gun and turned it on the three stowaways hiding behind the rack.

"Come out where I can see you," he ordered. "Hands in the air."

Aaron tucked his knife into his shoe and the three climbed out from behind the rack and stood facing Pankov.

Pankov looked at Uri, disgusted. "I am so glad I could count on you in a fight," he said sourly. "I thought you carried a damn *sidearm*."

Uri just stood there looking sheepish. "I do," he said.

Pankov found a roll of duct tape and tossed it to him. "Tie them up," he said. "Then meet me in the Control Center and prepare to dive."

"*Dive,* sir?" Uri said. "But we still have guests on board."

"The party is over for them, Captain," Pankov said. "Even *you* must know they have heard too much to be set free. The mission begins now!" He turned to leave.

"What about Ekatarina?" Uri said after him. "She's your daughter, sir."

Pankov stopped and looked back at Uri. "Are you going to follow orders, Captain? Or are you going to stand there looking like an idiot?"

Uri looked at the hostages, and for a moment he chose the latter, thinking that under the circumstances it was his best option. But as an experienced military officer he knew it would be safer to follow orders.

"Yes, sir, Comrade Captain," he said, standing straight.

He glanced at Fagan's body. "But we are severely undermanned now, sir."

Pankov took a deep breath in through his nose and exhaled out his mouth. "I am aware that we are *down* a man, Uri," he said. "What would you have me do? Call off the mission? Is that what you are asking me to do?"

"N-no, sir," Uri said stupidly.

Katya looked at Pankov with fear, disbelief, and tears in her eyes. He had become an evil stranger now, her mortal enemy, a dark shadow of the man who had raised her. "Why are you doing this, Father?" she said. "What's happened to you?"

Pankov ignored her and turned to Jason. "I am grateful there is *someone* in this room whose loyalty need not be questioned."

"Yes, sir," Jason said. He saw Brandy looking at him, and for a moment he looked back at her, but the overwhelming sadness in her eyes made him look away.

Pankov turned to Uri and said, "We'll be in the Control Center. Report there when you are finished. And do something about that body. We will need all the fresh air we can get."

He and Jason ducked out through the watertight hatch.

"You heard the man," Uri Ruden said. "Let's go." He indicated the starboard torpedo rack with a wave of his duct tape.

Aaron searched Uri's eyes for a moment, hoping to find a glimmer of compassion. But there was nothing there, so he turned toward the rack, feeling the barrel of a pistol jam into his lower back.

Uri directed the three hostages to sit together on the floor, and then he used the tape to tie them securely to the rack.

~ PART III ~

THE MISSION

Chapter 52

Ashley Quinn had heard what sounded like the terrifying, muffled sounds of fighting. Not knowing what else to do, she had stayed where she was, glued to her seat at the chart table in the Control Room, waiting nervously for her boyfriend to return.

She jumped when Jason and Pankov entered the compartment.

"Who are you?" Pankov said to her, not really expecting an answer. He stood at the helm and proceeded to go over his checklist.

Ashley had never seen Pankov before, and she was shocked by his battered and bleeding appearance.

"I-I'm Martha," she said. "I'm with Richard Fagan."

She looked at Jason. "Have you seen him?"

Jason glanced at Pankov, wondering how to answer that question.

"Commander Fagan is dead," Pankov said coldly.

Ashley's hand went to her throat. "What did you just say?" She looked at Jason in disbelief, but his expression confirmed that it was true.

"His emotions got the better of him," Jason said.

Ashley stared at him, incredulous, and then her vision went dark and she dropped to the floor.

Pankov looked at her as if she were a piece of discarded meat. "Whose idea was it to have a party tonight anyway?" he said.

"Commander Fagan thought of it, sir," Jason said.

"*That* worked out well."

"Yes, sir," Jason said.

"Put her in with the others," Pankov ordered. "And while you're at it, see what's taking Uri."

Jason scooped Ashley up off the floor and draped her over his shoulder, finding her surprisingly thin and frail. Her perfume was subtle but perfectly suited to her, and he found himself slightly aroused.

He carried her to the Forward Torpedo Room and peered in through the watertight hatch. Uri was just finishing tying Aaron, Katya, and Brandy to the torpedo rack with a tangle of duct tape.

"Give me a hand here, will you, Uri?" Jason said through the hatch.

Uri was surprised to see Jason carrying Martha over his shoulder. He helped him lift her through the tight opening, and they flopped her down next to Katya.

Aaron saw who it was, and that she was unconscious. "*What did you do to her?*" he demanded. "*If she's hurt, I swear to God I'll —*"

"Tie her up with the others," Jason said to Uri, ignoring Aaron. "Then report to the Control Room. Pankov's anxious to get moving."

"Can you at least give me a hand with Fagan? We don't want to be tripping over him."

"Okay, but let's hurry it up," Jason said.

Uri quickly tied Ashley up with the other hostages, and then he and Jason moved Fagan's body the length of the sub to Compartment Seven, the Aft Torpedo Room, where they shoved the corpse into a corner before heading back to the Control Room to join Pankov.

Chapter 53

Aaron looked over at his mother, but she was still unconscious. The four of them were alone in the Forward Torpedo Room, and Aaron knew he had to work fast. Brandy and Katya looked at him, hoping for a miracle.

He analyzed Uri's tie job and concluded that the man wasn't very good with duct tape. He easily worked a hand down to his shoe and retrieved his pocketknife.

He cut the tape on his wrists and legs and freed himself, and then he stepped out from behind the torpedo rack and walked over to torpedo tube 5 and opened the inner hatch cover.

"What about us?" Brandy said.

"We're not leaving here just yet," he said. "The timing's not right."

He used the gantry crane and pulley systems to remove the forest green, nuclear-warhead torpedo from the tube, replacing it with the red and white dummy torpedo.

Then he sat down next to the girls and taped himself to the rack in a way the made him appear to be securely tied, when he really wasn't. He kicked the duct tape away with his foot and tucked his pocketknife into his right hand.

"What do we do now?" Brandy asked.

"Now, we wait," Aaron said.

Chapter 54

Back in the Control Room, Pankov went over the mission plan with Uri and Jason one more time. He was counting on Jason's advice. With Richard Fagan dead, Jason's local knowledge would be critical to the success of the mission.

"We must allow plenty of time to navigate the shallow water near the docks without incident," Jason said. "Even at high tide, which we'll have, the water here near the Maritime Museum is only about twenty feet deep, so we won't be able to fully submerge until we reach the main channel, where the bottom drops off closer to fifty feet."

"We'll submerge the boat just enough to slip out from under the tarpaulin," Uri said. "Then we'll head for the channel."

"Agreed," Pankov said.

"There's a U.S. Coast Guard base just to the northwest," Jason said. "So we'll have to be very quiet, running silently on electric motors alone."

"Cobra's batteries are fully charged," Uri said.

"There's a shoal just west of the Coronado Ferry Landing and east of the carrier basin on the Coronado side of the bay," Jason said. "And another between the #1 green buoy and the amphibious base southeast at the entrance to Glorietta Bay. They can be trouble for large skimmers on average tides and even to smaller vessels at low tides. For us they would spell disaster on any tide."

"Understood," Pankov said. He rigged out one of the periscope's handles and rested his hand on it. "We will have no Navigator or Quartermaster, so I'll be guiding us using the attack periscope with whatever light is available. Jason, you will be my first officer. I'll need you by me at the helm and possibly in the Engine Room when Uri is otherwise occupied. Can you handle that?"

"Yes, sir," Jason said confidently. He was well trained in all aspects of submarine warfare.

Uri was disappointed. He had assumed that because of his and Pankov's long history together, *he* would be First Officer. But apparently his standing with Pankov had slipped down a notch after the Richard Fagan fiasco.

"Uri, you will act as Torpedo Officer and Diving Officer," Pankov said.

Uri was well qualified at those positions and had anticipated this. "Yes, sir," he said.

"Including myself, and with Fagan dead, we have three men with which to crew this boat," Pankov said. "I am aware that this will be nearly impossible, but I am left with no choice. It is not necessary for me to remind you that we have no medical officer. So keep your wits about you. I need able-bodied men, not casualties of war."

"Yes, sir," Uri said.

Jason didn't respond. As a ranking officer, he had always considered it a waste of time to be lectured about safety.

"Once submerged we will head southeast to the Coronado Bridge," Pankov said, "where we will remain hidden at periscope depth while we wait for the *Neau Islander*. Are there any questions?"

"No, sir," the men said.

"All right then," Pankov said. "Our time has come, Gentlemen. Let us get underway."

Uri's first task as Diving Officer was to monitor the hull opening indicator lights. Once the green lights showed all hull openings closed, he bled compressed air into the ship. When the internal air pressure remained constant, he knew that watertight integrity was assured.

"Depth below keel?" Pankov said.

"Two-and-a-half meters, sir," Jason said. "We'll have to belly crawl our way out of here."

"Shift to battery," Pankov ordered. "Close fin hatch and open motor room doors and air locks. Port and starboard motors slow reverse."

Jason engaged the electric motors and Pankov slowly backed Cobra out from under the white tarpaulin.

Aaron felt the sub lurch backward and he glanced around the Forward Torpedo Room. "I think we're *moving*," he said, keeping his voice low. The girls looked at each other in agreement.

Aaron's throat went dry as suddenly his escape plan was thrown out the window.

Just then Ashley jerked awake, looking around. "W-what happened?" she said groggily. Aaron looked at her hopefully, but she still didn't know him from Adam.

"Prepare to dive," Pankov ordered. "Close snorkel ... close diesel exhaust valve. Sound dive alarm and dive to one-and-a-half meters; 5 degree trim on bow, course 180 degrees. Up periscope."

Jason and Uri scrambled to keep up with Pankov's rapid fire orders.

I knew we couldn't do this with three crewmen, Uri thought bitterly.

"Port and Starboard motors slow forward," Pankov said. "Open Kingston Valve Bow and Stern Group Ballast Tanks. Open Ventilation Valve Bow and Stern Group Ballast Tanks. Open Kingston Valve Middle Group Ballast Tanks. Open Ventilation Valve Middle Group Ballast Tanks. Extend Forward Dive Planes."

"Depth one and a half meters, sir," Jason said.

"Close Ventilation Valves," Pankov said. "Maintain present depth. Down all masts."

Navigating by periscope, Pankov sailed Cobra slowly away from the docks, arcing around the Midway Aircraft Carrier and out into the main channel of San Diego Bay.

"Depth below keel?" Pankov said.

Jason was relieved to finally see some water under them. "Nine meters, Captain."

"Open Ventilation Valves," Pankov said. "Dive to seven meters, 5 degree trim on bow, come left 15 degrees."

His skeleton crew did as ordered and Cobra submerged for the first time in twenty years.

"I hope she holds up, Captain," Uri Ruden said as they dropped below the surface. The creaking of corroded steel and the appearance of numerous small leaks made him wonder.

Pankov rested his hand fondly on one of Cobra's steel bulkheads. "She may be old, Uri, but she's sturdy," he assured him. "Jason, what is the sounding?"

"Five meters below keel, Captain."

"Increase speed to one-third. Come left 30 degrees and level off at periscope depth. Adjust fore-and-aft trim."

Pankov steered Cobra southeast toward the Coronado Bridge, where he instructed his crew to turn the sub 180 degrees, facing them north, toward the cruise ship *Neau Islander*.

"All stop!" he ordered.

"*Aaron?*" Katya asked, startled. "Am I imagining things, or is there more water in here than there used to be?"

Aaron saw that she was right. There was a sizable crack somewhere in the pressure hull, and seawater was flooding in. They had to get the hell out of the Forward Torpedo Room, and soon.

Chapter 55

Captain Zaane stood in *Neau Islander's* wheelhouse checking his watch. 8:09 p.m.

"All right, gentlemen," he said to his officers. "Let's be underway."

The First Officer gave the order.

PHOOOOOOOOOOT!

Even at that distance, and at periscope depth, Pankov could hear that Captain Zaane was preparing to sail. He checked his watch. 8:10 p.m.

Within a few minutes he heard the ship's horn sound again.

PHOOOOOT! PHOOOOOT! PHOOOOOT!

The triple blast indicated that the huge cruise ship was backing away from the dock. Pankov put his eye to the periscope and waited until he spotted *Neau Islander* heading slowly out past the Midway Aircraft Carrier.

He checked his watch. 8:25 on the nose. *Very impressive, Captain Zaane,* he thought, smiling to himself.

A rush of adrenaline surged through him, a rush he hadn't felt since the Cuban Missile Crisis back in 1962. *This* was where he was happiest, here surrounded by skilled officers, working together to achieve a common goal. This was where Captain Vtorak Borisovich Pankov of the Soviet Navy belonged.

"All ahead one-third," he ordered.

Chapter 56

Pankov skillfully maneuvered Cobra beneath *Neau Islander's* tremendous prop-wash. The turbulence shook the old submarine like a rubber duck in a Jacuzzi, as new leaks popped up all around him.

"Steady at periscope depth," Pankov said as they followed Captain Zaane west toward the nuclear submarine base near the mouth of the harbor.

"There are shoaling waters to starboard, Captain," Jason cautioned. "Be especially careful when nearing the southern tip of Shelter Island. Stay directly behind the cruise ship and keep us *off* the bottom."

As they neared Ballast Point, Pankov spotted the bait barges through the scope, followed by the large security floats surrounding the nuclear submarine base.

He gave the order to slow, and the turbulence stopped as Zaane and his *Neau Islander* continued on out of the harbor and into the Pacific Ocean.

Maintaining periscope depth, and constant visual contact with the submarine base, Pankov slid Cobra under the long row of bait barges.

He checked his watch. 8:55 p.m.

"Gentlemen," he said. "Prepare to fire."

Chapter 57

Uri Ruden ran to the Forward Torpedo Room to prepare tube 5 for firing. He ducked through the watertight hatch and was alarmed when his feet splashed into a foot of rising water. He froze for a moment, knowing he should inform Pankov immediately.

Aaron saw his chance and leaped out from behind the torpedo rack, sinking the 3-inch blade of his pocket survival knife deep into Uri's back. Uri lurched forward, blood spewing from his mouth, reaching desperately behind his back trying to identify the offending object.

The girls recoiled in horror and struggled against their bindings.

Aaron had hoped to pierce Uri's heart but had hit a lung instead. He pulled the knife out with a stiff jerk and drove it deep again. This time blood gushed over the knife handle and Aaron knew the blade had hit home. He braced himself and gripped hard, pulling his knife free, as Uri splashed lifeless into the rising seawater.

Breathing hard and soaked to the skin, Aaron stepped back and wiped the blade on his thigh. The girls stared at him in disbelief.

He quickly folded the knife into his pocket and then scrabbled around underwater for Uri's gun, whacking it on his thigh several times to remove any excess water.

"I'm taking us to the Captain's Cabin," he said to the others. "We'll be as safe there as anywhere until I figure out what the hell to do."

Then, at last, to their infinite relief, he cut the girls loose.

Naval Base Point Loma
San Diego

Chapter 58

Commander Adam Byrd stood on the bridge of the nuclear submarine, USS *Hampton.* He checked his wristwatch. 8:50 p.m.

He waited as the massive cruise ship *Neau Islander* slowly cleared Ballast Point, and then, at precisely 9:00 p.m., he maneuvered his billion-dollar vessel, along with its priceless cargo, the President of the United States, carefully out into San Diego Bay.

Suddenly the boat's chief sonar operator's eyes went wide as something unexpected came into his headphones. For a second he thought it was a *submarine.*

"Sir, I think you need to hear this," he said.

Byrd stepped over and put one of the phones to his ear, but as quickly as it had appeared, the strange sound was gone.

"Sorry, sir," the operator said. "False alarm. Something must have come loose on one of the bait barges."

"Stay on it, Chief," Byrd said. "Considering who we have on board tonight, I'd rather have a hundred false alarms than no alarms at all."

"Yes, sir," the operator said.

Pankov watched through Cobra's attack periscope. "Where the hell's Uri?" he said to Jason. "We'll be ready to fire soon!"

Jason had spent years in the Navy perfecting his submarine warfare skills, and he didn't need Uri's help.

"We can do it without him, Captain," he said. "The torpedo is armed and loaded in tube five. I just need to open the outer hatch, flood the tube, and prime the high pressure air system."

"Make it happen," Pankov said. "Go!"

Jason sprinted down the corridor to the Forward Torpedo Room leaving all of the hatches open behind him.

He was shocked to find Uri Ruden's body floating in the rising water, and that Aaron and the girls were gone, but he quickly gathered himself and prepared tube 5 for firing. "Fire when ready, sir!" he shouted down the corridor.

Pankov checked the scope. The *Hampton* was dead ahead.

"*FIRE!*" he shouted back.

"Firing, sir!" Jason shouted back.

Jason pulled the chrome firing lever and there was a low shudder as a blast of compressed air forced the torpedo out of tube 5 just as the weapon's self-propulsion system kicked on.

Pankov braced himself for a nuclear explosion and certain death, using a stop watch to count it down. Based upon the range, he was expecting the rocket propelled nuke to impact the *Hampton* in under four seconds.

Three ...

Two ...

One ...

Nothing!

Pankov was horrified. Had they missed?

He waited a few more seconds, but he knew it was true: Through one evil stroke of incomprehensibly bad luck, the shot had been a colossal dud.

The USS *Hampton's* chief sonar operator's eyes went wide again. But before he could react, his eardrums were split by a huge metallic *BANG!* as the massive nuclear submarine was impacted by a heavy foreign object. The brutal hit shook the entire ship, knocking dozens of seamen off their feet and echoing on for several seconds.

"*All stop!*" Commander Byrd shouted from the bridge. He remained steady and calm, not wanting to cause a panic. He grabbed hold of the periscope's training handles and took a quick scan around the area.

The President and his agents were off somewhere touring the sub and he wasn't hooked up to his safety line yet. He grabbed hold of an overhead pipe to keep from hitting the deck, looking around nervously as his Secret Service team jumped into high alert.

Commander Byrd took his Executive Officer aside. "What the hell was that?" he said in a near whisper. "Did we *hit* something?"

"I think something hit *us*," the XO replied. "And it struck our port side, Captain, from *inside* the bay. Perhaps it was a shark or a dolphin, sir."

Byrd gave him a look that said, *Please tell me my XO's not that stupid ...*

"Damage report!"

"No damage to report, sir!" was the reply.

"The President?"

"The President is unharmed, sir!"

"Sonar! What *was* that?"

"I-I don't know, Captain," the operator replied, still shaking, his ears ringing. "It came out of nowhere. It sounded like — a *torpedo*."

"If someone is firing at us they're shooting blanks," Byrd said.

"By the sound of it, it had to weigh close to a ton, sir," the operator said.

Byrd paused for a moment, looking at the sonar operator. "Let's say it *was* a torpedo, Chief. Where would it have come from?"

"From under the bait barges, sir," the operator said.

"Is there even enough *room* under there for a submarine?" Byrd asked.

"That's on the bay side of us, Captain," the XO said, stepping in confidently. "Anyone hiding there would never have gotten past us in the first place."

"You're probably right, Commander," Byrd said. "But, for the sake of argument, let's say that they did. Could they hide something as big as submarine under the *bait barges?*"

"It's highly unlikely, Captain," the XO said. "An older diesel, maybe. But we haven't seen one of those in these waters for several years. And we would certainly have detected them as they entered the bay."

Byrd pictured the old Russian submarine, b-39, moored at the MMSD at the east end of the harbor, but he quickly filed the thought away with all of his other ridiculous ideas. It did, however, make him wonder: "What if it *was* a diesel-electric," he said. "Our enemies are buying them up like they're going out of style. I've heard the Iranians have *seventeen* of the damn things."

"But don't you think we would have *heard* them, Captain?" the XO said, stressing his earlier point.

"There's no doubt that the U.S. Navy's anti-submarine warfare capabilities are the best in the business, Commander," Byrd said. "However, as you know, with variations in the underwater topography, ambient noise generated by marine life and merchant shipping, and changing salinity and temperatures, all of which alter how sounds propagate, it is still very difficult for us to combat diesel-electric submarines running silently on battery power. Hell, with all the other noise in the bay, it's like trying to detect a single taxi cab in downtown *Manhattan*."

Captain Byrd knew he had made his point, but he also knew how important it was to him and the rest of his crew that this VIP cruise come off without a hitch. His sub appeared to have sustained no significant damage, and the minute they returned to port he would have the exterior of the hull inspected to confirm. As for the enemy sub? He chose not to believe there ever was one. And he knew they needed to get moving again soon, if they were to have any chance of completing this all important drill.

He took his Executive Officer aside again, speaking in a low voice. "I think under the circumstances we should just file this incident in the ghost file."

"I have to agree, Captain," the XO said. "What else can we do, with the goddamn President on board and all?"

"Easy, Commander," Byrd said. "He *is* our Commander-in-chief, don't forget."

"Sorry, Captain," the XO said. "I guess the stress is taking its toll. It won't happen again."

"See that it doesn't, Commander," Byrd said.

Suddenly the agent with the carnation appeared on the bridge, frantic for information. "What was that horrendous sound?" he demanded, looking at Commander Byrd as if he had been personally responsible. "I was with the President, and we were very close to the source. It was *deafening*."

"Nothing unusual, Agent," Byrd replied calmly, sharing Fagan's disdain for Secret Service agents. "Just the hull shifting under pressure. It's very common at sea. Nothing to worry about."

The agent's eyes narrowed. *That was pretty damn loud to be a hull shift,* he thought. But he knew he had no choice but to pass Captain Byrd's explanation on to the President. He turned and headed off to give his report.

Byrd picked up a mic and his entire crew heard the following over the intercom: *"This your Captain speaking. I know that what just occurred onboard the USS Hampton may seem strange or even frightening to some of you. However, I can assure you that everything is under control. We are professional submariners, and we shall act accordingly. Proceed with the Emergency Nighttime Surface Drill. Captain out."*

He replaced the mic.

Jason was just outside Cobra's Forward Torpedo Room. He shouted down the corridor to the Control Room. "What the hell happened, Captain? Did we miss?"

"You loaded the wrong *goddamn torpedo!*" Pankov shouted back.

"That's *impossible*," Jason shouted. "Uri loaded the damn thing himself!"

"Obviously he screwed up!" Pankov yelled. "Now shut up and load the *live* one, damn it!"

Jason knew it too late, the flooding was getting worse, and the USS *Hampton* was probably long gone anyway. Purely out of curiosity, he went back to take a look at the torpedo that was still on the rack.

But what he saw there was not the conventional weapon Uri had described. It was a forest green torpedo with the markings: *VA-111 Shkval.*

It was a goddamn *nuke!*

That's why Fagan was fighting with Pankov when I shot him, Jason thought miserably. *He found the nuke. He knew that Pankov and Uri were planning a damn suicide mission!*

Chapter 59

Aaron knew he had to make his move. He figured his mother, Katya, and Brandy were safer with him than alone in the Captain's Cabin, so he gathered them together and moved cautiously out and down the corridor toward the Control Room.

The flooding was out of control, now, and even Pankov knew they had to abort the mission. But in his crazed state he was certain they could pick up where they left off at a later date — if only he could save his beloved submarine.

"Forget the torpedo, Jason," he yelled down the corridor. *"Blow main ballast. Flank speed! We need to surface!"*

Jason heard him, and did his best to make that happen.

Aaron had the girls wait in the corridor while he entered the Control Room alone. Pankov was hunched over the helm trying desperately to make something happen. He looked up briefly — Aaron stiffened and started to go for his knife — then returned to the controls, ignoring him.

Aaron gestured to the others, hoping that they weren't too deep and that he and the girls could climb the ladder to the fin hatch and escape.

He felt a shake and heard the sounds of Cobra's propellers struggling to drive the sub to the surface; but her old batteries were weak and the electric motors were unable to overcome the weight of the seawater filling the pressure hull.

Suddenly the sounds stopped, followed by a low, metallic groan, like the bellow of a great, iron demon from a cavern in hell. The submarine drifted slowly downward, tilting slightly on its side before hitting the mud on the bottom of the bay with a tremendous *WHUUMPP!*

Aaron and the girls were knocked off their feet, splashing into water that was now almost knee deep.

Pankov held on and managed to remain at the helm, his hair wet and falling in his eyes. Chilling seawater sprayed in from every direction with a deafening roar.

Aaron stood and helped the girls to their feet. "*Can't we surface?*" he shouted to Pankov.

"Didn't you *hear that?*" Pankov yelled back. "We're on the bottom! The engines have quit! The electrical has shorted out! We're taking on water like a sieve, and we have no compressed air to blow ballast! A damn cinder block would have a better chance of making it to the surface!" He turned away and put his gun to his head.

"*No!*" Katya cried, running to him.

POP!

The lead entered Pankov's right temple, followed by a gush of blood, and he fell backward into the rising flood.

Katya watched her father sink beneath the churning waters, never to breathe air again. She turned and looked at Aaron, her eyes filled with the kind of horror only a grieving daughter could know, and then she collapsed in his arms.

Aaron held Katya close, looking desperately at his mother. He had hoped that before they died, she would learn the truth: that her only son had *not* been killed but had lived through the crash after all. He knew in his heart that that was all she'd need to snap her out of the amnesia and bring her back where she belonged ... with him.

But they were running out of time.

Chapter 60

Brandy stood in the back of the Control Room, staring blankly at the others. Her dress was drenched and clinging to her skin like tissue paper, and she was in a state of shock. Along with everything else that had happened to them tonight, this was too much to take on.

Suddenly a hand closed over her mouth and another gripped her arm, and she was hauled violently down through the watertight hatch leading to Compartment Two.

Brandy struggled with all of her strength as Jason pulled her down the corridor and threw her into the Captain's Cabin; but instead of hurting her, he backed her against the wall and kissed her passionately on the mouth.

Frightened and confused, Brandy kissed him back, and for a brief, glorious moment she thought he really meant it. Everything else in her chaotic world vanished, as she lost herself completely in him.

But then came a frightening, sickening, excruciating pain in her abdomen. A pain like she had never known or begun to imagine. She opened her mouth to scream, but Jason covered it with his hand, using the other to yank his knife out of her stomach. He stepped aside to avoid the gush of blood, and then let her fall on the bunk where she lay looking up at him.

Why did you do this Jason? she pleaded silently. *What could I possibly have done that would make you do this?*

Jason looked down at her, seawater dripping from his hair and clothing. He wiped the sharp blade on his wet thigh and turned to leave.

He stopped and looked back at her. "Before I go," he said. "There's something I've been meaning to tell you."

Brandy saw the evil that was coming and her eyes narrowed. *Let me die in peace, you sick bastard.*

"My last name isn't really Beckham," he said. "I assumed that name after being kicked out of the Navy. My birth name is Souther. I'm Johnny's brother."

Brandy stared at him, utter disbelief momentarily masking her pain. But what Jason had just told her was far too cruel to be a lie. The bastard had lived a lie, and he would die a liar ... but for once she knew he was telling the truth.

"There's something I've been meaning to tell you as well, Jason," she said. "You'll never be *half* the man your brother was."

Jason faked a smile and then turned and left the room.

Brandy tried to sit up and call for help, but she was far too weak and only managed a feeble moan.

Chapter 61

Aaron held Katya tightly, not knowing how to comfort a girl who just witnessed her own father's suicide.

He turned to look at Brandy, who'd been standing by the open hatch where they had come in, but she was gone.

"Keep Katya here with you," he said to his mother, handing Ekatarina to her, and then he ducked through the hatch into Compartment Two.

Aaron splashed down the corridor, quickly checking each of the rooms, and when he checked the Captain's Cabin he saw Brandy lying on the bunk with a wound to the stomach, blood soaking her dress and the blanket on which she lay.

Of all the people on earth, there was no one she would rather have seen walk through that door. She managed a weak smile and held out her hand, speaking just above a whisper.

"Aaron ..."

Aaron squeezed her hand, and then he pulled off his shirt and used it to help stop the bleeding, but Brandy's face was pale; she had clearly lost a lot of blood already. All he could think to do was make her as comfortable as possible. He sat next to her on the bunk and took her hand. "Lie still, Brandy. You're going to be all right."

She looked up at him and spoke in the calm voice. "People used to ask me why I was always attracted to the weird ones," she said. "I never really knew how to answer that question."

Jason did this, Aaron thought, and a rage unlike any he had ever known swelled in his breast.

She squeezed his hand. "I love you Aaron," she said.

He looked at her for a long moment. "I love you, too, Brandy."

"Katya told me about your ordeal with Johnny Souther," she said, "and that answers a lot of my questions about you. But there's something you need to know about me." She turned and coughed into the blanket. "My name's not really Brandy Fine. I-it's Barbara Fischer. Johnny renamed me after we first met."

"You know *Johnny Souther?*" Aaron said.

"We were lovers," Brandy said, gritting her teeth in pain. "We lived together until the day he died."

Aaron was suddenly outside Sally's Diner again as he and Willy pulled the triggers on their assault rifles and watched Johnny Souther die in a shower of glass.

"Th-there's one more thing," Brandy said. "Jason told me his last name isn't Beckham. It's Souther. He's Johnny's brother."

Aaron's brain nearly shut down. All the time he had spent with Jason, the weeks at sea, the bars, the cafés — the *camaraderie*. How could he have been so *stupid?*

"Jason told me Johnny was dead when he found him," Brandy said, "but I think he's the one who *killed* him."

What? No, Aaron thought. *I'm the one who killed him.*

Then, with a rush, it all dawned on him: *Jason was the one driving the black Hummer!*

Brandy took hold of Aaron's arm and looked him in the eye. "Promise me, Aaron," she said. "If it's the last thing you do on this earth ..."

But then she was gone.

Rest easy my dear friend, he thought, touching her shoulder. *That's exactly what I'm planning to do.*

He stood and went in search of Jason Souther.

Chapter 62

The water was thigh high as Aaron splashed through the hatch into the Control Room. More icy water sprayed in on him from every direction, and footing was difficult and progress slow due to the now steeply sloping deck.

For a brief, terrifying moment, the lights went out, and when they blinked on again, Aaron saw, to his horror, that Jason had somehow gotten past him and was standing near the helm controls holding Ashley and Katya at gunpoint.

Jason's back was turned, and with his free hand he was trying desperately to restart the electric motors. Aaron wanted to blow Jason's brains out, but Ashley and Katya were too near to his line of fire.

The girls saw him and wanted to call out to him, but he shook his head and held a finger to his lips, and then moved slowly over and pointed his pistol at the back of Jason's head.

"You and your brother are the reason I have no family!" Aaron said.

Jason froze for a long moment, and then suddenly he jerked to the side, grabbing Katya and backing off with his gun to her head. "What are you talking about?" he said. "Johnny's *dead*."

"*I'm the one who killed him,*" Aaron said.

Jason looked carefully at Aaron. "Wait a minute," he said. "You were at Sally's Diner that night. You left in an Aston Martin DBS."

"And you're the one that hit us and ran!" Aaron cried.

"What? I may have saved your life!" Jason said. "We were halfway to the hospital before the cops came and fucked everything up!"

Ashley Quinn's hand went to her mouth and she stared at Aaron in disbelief. Tears filled her eyes as a flood of memories rocked her senses and she was overwhelmed with both sorrow and joy. She had wanted so badly to remember ... She had wanted so badly to know who the young man named Aaron really was.

Aaron glanced at her and his heart stopped. Through her tears he could see the clear light of understanding in her eyes.

His mother was back.

Suddenly the submarine's pressure hull thumped and squealed as another rusted bulkhead weld gave way to the pressure.

Jason shoved Katya aside and fired. Ashley screamed as the bullet grazed the thin flesh covering Aaron's ribs. He staggered back and fired just as Jason ducked through the watertight hatch to Compartment Four.

"Head for the Forward Torpedo Room," he told the girls. "I'll meet you there."

He went after Jason.

Ashley felt a rush of adrenaline as her motherly instincts returned with a vengeance. She spotted a large pipe wrench on a shelf and picked it up. It had a good weight to it.

"I'm going with him," she said.

Katya hefted her own heavy piece of iron. "So am I. If we're going to die tonight ... it may as well be in a fight!"

Jason ran through Compartments 4, 5 and 6, all the way to the stern of the boat, Compartment Seven, the Aft Torpedo Room.

He climbed to the top of the compartment, frantically trying to get out through the escape hatch. But, to his dismay, instead of repairing it, the workmen had simply welded it shut.

Just then Aaron peered in through the watertight hatch.

Jason saw him and fired, the bullet ricocheting off the steel ring, inches from Aaron's face.

Aaron fired back and missed.

Suddenly a large pressure valve blew, spraying water like a fireman's hose, knocking Jason off his feet.

Aaron saw him go down and stepped inside the room with him. The water was waist deep now and spraying everywhere, making it difficult to move.

The lights blinked out again and then flickered back on.

Jason found his feet and spotted Aaron. He fired and missed.

Aaron had a clear shot and pulled the trigger, but his gun just *clicked*.

Jason knew it immediately and turned to fire.

Aaron dove underwater and came up catching him from behind. They tumbled into the water and Jason grabbed Aaron by the hair and held him down, leaning hard, using his full weight to shove him deeper underwater. Aaron kicked and twisted, unable to catch a breath, hair tearing from his scalp, but his opponent was too powerful.

Suddenly something struck Jason on the back of his skull, shattering his vision with a burst of blinding white light. Dazed, he lost his grip on Aaron and turned in time to see Katya taking another arcing swing at him with her heavy pipe. He caught the blow with his hand and wrenched the pipe from her grip, knocking her backward into the black, swirling water.

Aaron surfaced, sputtering and coughing, while behind him Jason raised the pipe high.

"*AARON!*" Ashley shouted through the din.

Aaron looked up just as his mother tossed the pipe wrench, catching it with one hand, while Jason's blow glanced painfully off his shoulder. He spun around with all the force he could muster, smashing Jason high in the throat. Blood spewed from between Jason's clenched teeth as reflex sent his hand to his crushed larynx. In disbelief he looked squarely at Aaron, then his eyes rolled up, and he fell face first into the rising water.

Chapter 63

Katya and Ashley stood dazed, waist deep in bloody seawater, being hit from all sides by the relentless, freezing spray. Aaron gathered them into his arms and held them for a long moment.

Just then the lights went out. Katya screamed, cowering back in disgusted horror. Something in the dark water had bumped into her hip.

The lights blinked on again, and Aaron saw that it was Fagan's dead body, its flesh gray and swollen. He tried to turn Katya away, but she saw it and screamed again, causing Ashley to scream as well.

"Let's get the hell out of here," Aaron shouted through the deafening spray, and at last they headed out of the Aft Torpedo Room.

Aaron swung the watertight hatch cover closed, sealing them off from the massive flow of water, but the Electric Motor Room was flooding as well now. Sparks arced and spit from the huge motors and control panels, and Aaron was concerned that they would all be electrocuted.

They moved on, passing through the Engine Room and Machinery Control Room before climbing the short stairway into Compartment Four, where they were out of the deepest water for a moment. Boxes of rice and other food items floated in the water near the Galley, as they moved along the tilted corridor.

They stepped through the watertight hatch into Compartment Three, and Aaron closed and sealed that hatch as well.

For a moment he just stood there, looking around the Control Room, casting desperately about for an idea — any idea. There *had* to be a way out of this. The air was thick and heavy, smelling of diesel oil and burnt wiring, becoming more and more difficult to breathe.

He looked up into the conning tower, but he knew that with the weight of half the bay sitting on top of it, he'd never be able to get the fin hatch open without first flooding the submarine to equalize the pressure.

Just then the boat shuddered as its bow rose slightly. The stern was filling with water, leaving an air pocket toward the bow. Aaron knew they would have air as long as they kept moving toward the front of the ship.

He saw a coil of rope hanging near the chart table, and suddenly an idea came to him. It was crazy, and extremely risky, but it was all he had.

He steeled himself and grabbed the rope, draping it over his shoulder. Then he looked at the shivering girls.

"I think I have a plan," he said, sounding as confident as he could. "Are you guys ready to get out of here?"

There was a light in Aaron's eyes they hadn't seen in a while, and they nodded hopefully.

"All right," he said. "Follow me."

Chapter 64

The second their flight touched down at San Diego International, Harness placed a call to Naval Command in Point Loma.

"Who did you say this was?" the receptionist asked, her tone arrogant and patronizing.

"I'm Detective James Harness," he repeated, slower this time. "I work in a small precinct on the East Coast."

"And what's this regarding?" she said.

"I'd rather speak to someone higher up. This is a matter of national security."

"I'm sorry, but I can't transfer you till I know what this is regarding."

"It's about a possible assassination attempt on the President," Harness said impatiently. "We're wasting precious time here. It's happening as we speak!"

"Hold please," the receptionist said, and she was gone.

Harness waited for what felt like an hour. He was just about to hang up when the receptionist returned to the line, sounding like a digital recording. Harness could not get a word in edgewise.

"We appreciate your concern," she said. "However, I've been instructed to assure you that sufficient security has been arranged for the President's visit. If you have any further questions or concerns you may try our website at ..." She gave Harness a complicated website address and hung up.

"*Damn it*," Harness mumbled to himself. "I'm an officer of the law ... and they couldn't care less."

He briefly considered calling the SDPD, but he knew that dealing with another bureaucracy and another patronizing receptionist would cost him valuable time. And he'd lost too much time already.

Darkness had settled on the city when Harness and Holt took a cab from the airport to the Maritime Museum of San Diego, and when they jumped out and ran down to where b-39 should have been, they were surprised to see nothing but a huge, white plastic tarp.

"What the hell is this all about?" Harness said.

They crossed the wooden gangplank, and when they pulled back the flap they discovered that the entire submarine was *missing*.

Very clever, Harness thought, admiring the ingenuity. *Enclose the sub in a weathertight shelter, and no one will ever know you're gone.*

He spotted the Zodiac tied up to the dock and threw a glance at Holt.

Holt gave him a look that said, *No way, Detective. I'm not going out on that huge bay in the dark in that thing!*

"If you've got a better idea, I'm all ears," Harness said.

Holt didn't.

"After you," Harness said.

They stepped into the Zodiac and headed off across the black waters of San Diego Bay.

Chapter 65

The ship continued to tilt upward and to the side, and as Aaron, Ashley, and Katya moved toward the bow they faced a steep, awkward incline. The sub was almost totally flooded now, and it seemed that no matter how high they climbed they were always waist deep in seawater.

At last they reached the bow of the ship, and the hatch leading to Compartment One, the Forward Torpedo Room. They ducked inside and Aaron cranked the hatch cover closed.

The water was only knee deep there, and at first Aaron thought it wasn't rising, but he was wrong. It was rising faster than ever.

Aaron found it harder to breathe in there, as well, as if all of the bad air from the entire submarine had been compressed into the small space they were in. He tried to breath only through his mouth, but it didn't work. *We're running out of oxygen*, he thought, panic teasing his insides.

He looked around and found the Submerged Escape Apparatus hanging where he and Uri had seen it earlier. He removed it from its hook and turned to the girls.

"Here's the plan," he said. "This is a rescue breather — a lung for breathing underwater. We're going to use it to swim out through the torpedo tube."

The girls looked at him as if he'd gone completely insane.

"Can we *do that?*" Ashley asked.

"To be honest, I'm not really sure," Aaron said quickly. "All I know is, I read about a guy who did it once and lived to talk about it."

The freezing seawater had risen to waist deep, and the girls huddled together in a vain attempt to keep warm.

The lights continued to flicker dangerously, threatening to cut out once and for all. Aaron knew that if he and the girls were plunged into total darkness before he was ready, they were done for.

He checked the lung; the gauge indicated that it still had a small amount of oxygen in it. "This lung is very old, and won't be very effective," he said. "So we'll have to move fast."

"Th-that's the only one?" Katya said, shivering uncontrollably now.

"Yes," Aaron said. "You two will have to share."

"But what about you?" Ashley said.

"I'll be fine," Aaron said quickly, and he could only pray that that was true.

He gave the girls a quick demonstration on the use of the lung. "Just breathe into this mouthpiece. The air will come automatically."

The girls looked at the device doubtfully.

"And no matter what happens," he said, "don't follow me into the tube until I signal you, okay?"

The girls nodded.

Aaron showed Katya the button that would open the torpedo tube's outer door. "Remember, don't open the door until the seawater level reaches the top of the tube," he said. "We have to fill this compartment enough to flood the entire tube, if we're going to have any chance of equalizing the pressure."

"Understood," Katya said.

The water level was rapidly rising, and the lights continued to blink off and on, making it nearly impossible for Aaron to concentrate. He handed one end of the rope to Ashley, tying the other end around his waist, and then, saying a quick prayer, crawled into the tube.

Space was tight there in the tube. The only thing Aaron could get a grip on were the thin lands, raised strips of steel running the length of the tube. He muscled his way to the muzzle end and grabbed hold of the crossbar that stiffened the tube's outer door.

At last the water in the torpedo room reached the level of the tube. Aaron felt the change in pressure in his ears, and what little light he had was pushed out as the cold bay water rushed in, filled the tube, chilling him to the bone.

He took one last breath and held on to the crossbar as the water swirled in over his head. The darkness was complete.

Press the button, he thought. *Come on Katya, the tube is full, girl ... I need for you to press the button.*

The cold, watery blackness inside the tube was intolerably close. Panic gripped Aaron's heart and tried to rip it from his chest, and he was certain this hellish, black-steel tube would be his grave.

Suddenly, with banging rush, the muzzle door opened. Aaron held tight to the crossbar and he was drawn part way out of the tube's mouth. Lungs bursting, he thrust his arms outside and pulled his body through into the dark freezing waters of the bay. It had been half a minute since his last breath.

The girls had climbed up the torpedo rack in order to breathe in the small pocket of air that remained.

Ashley felt Aaron tug on the rope. "*That's the signal!*"

Suddenly the Forward Torpedo Room went dark as the last of the reserve power shorted out.

The two women groped desperately for each other in the terrifying blackness, the choking seawater up to their necks.

At last Katya's hand found Ashley's face. "*Are you with me, Ashley?*" she cried, spitting water by the cupful.

"I'm here," Ashley coughed. "*Let's do it!*"

Summoning every last ounce of their willpower, they gulped what would likely be their last breaths and ducked under the icy black water.

Darkness covered the entire bay now. Harness could barely see ten feet in front of the Zodiac.

They had decided to head for the nuclear submarine base at Point Loma first, but they had motored almost all the way to Ballast Point without seeing *anything*. And as they cruised past the row of bait barges, little did they know that forty feet below them, Aaron, Katya, and Ashley were fighting for their lives.

The men continued on out toward the mouth of the bay, venturing a short distance into the Pacific Ocean.

To the south, a few miles off shore, they could see the distant lights of a cruise ship, most likely heading for Cabo, but the USS *Hampton* was long gone, and Cobra was nowhere to be seen.

Holt's head hurt from peering into the darkness. "It's been an hour already and I ain't seen nothin'," he said.

"You're right," Harness said. "Let's head back up the bay and take one more look."

And at that point they turned around.

Katya went first, feeling her way into the dark, narrow torpedo tube, blindly following the rope, while clutching the rescue breather to her breast. Ashley scrambled in immediately behind her, and she, too, used the rope as her only guide.

Aaron's head and lungs were about to explode, his eyes close to popping from their sockets. But he held tight to the rope.

Come on guys, he thought desperately, *You can do it! Be strong, ladies! Be strong!*

Katya squeezed as far into the tube as she could, waiting for Ashley's hands touch her feet, and then she tugged hard on the rope. Aaron quickly took up the slack and then braced his feet on the sub's outer hull. Then, with everything he had, he started pulling the rope toward himself hand over hand. It had been over a minute since his last breath.

At last, just as Aaron was about to black out, Katya emerged from the tube holding the lung. She took a quick breath and then feeling in the dark she passed the lung to Aaron, who took two quick breaths before passing it back and pulling Ashley through. Katya took another big hit and then she found Ashley's face and pressed the mask over her mouth, forcing her to take a lifesaving breath of her own.

Finally, due to Aaron's skill and wealth of diving experience, the three escapees managed to buddy breathe their way through a cold, dark, disorienting, and terrifyingly long ascent to the surface.

They came up together, splashing, choking, and gasping for air.

Aaron quickly got his bearings. They had drifted into the middle of the harbor and were facing a long swim in every direction. The girls were clearly nearing exhaustion, unable to tread water much longer.

Suddenly, out of the darkness, an inflatable outboard came racing toward them from the south, and for a desperate moment the survivors thought they'd been spotted.

They yelled and screamed and waved and splashed with everything they had, but soon it became clear that on its present course, their best hope of rescue would pass them forever.

Detective Harness held on as the Zodiac bounded across the bay, his eyes straining to see through the blackness.

Suddenly he saw what looked like a commotion on the water. He looked again — there were *swimmers* in the water, and they were in trouble.

"*Come about, Holt, hard to port!*" he shouted.

Holt yanked on the tiller and the Zodiac arced hard left.

"Hold her on course," Harness commanded. "We have three swimmers dead ahead."

He grabbed the boat's only two life vests from under his seat and prepared to throw.

Chapter 66

The toss was perfect, the life vests landing within reach of all three swimmers.

Aaron made sure his companions had a firm grip, and then he grabbed a handful of the orange canvas for himself.

Holt pulled the boat up next to them and set the prop to neutral.

"Is anyone injured?" Harness said, doing a quick assessment.

Aaron looked at his companions and determined that other than being severely hypothermic and nearly drowned, everyone was in one piece.

"We're okay," he said quickly. "Please, help the ladies first." Holt used his superior strength to haul the girls on board.

Harness gave Aaron a hand up, and in spite of the darkness he recognized him immediately. "Aaron Quinn?" he said. "Is that you?"

Aaron stared back at him for a long moment. "Detective Harness?" he said at last, both shocked and extremely happy to recognize his friend.

"We stayed away as long as we could," Harness quipped. "But after cruising the harbor for over an hour, we got bored."

"Thanks for nothing," Aaron said, and shook Harness's hand gratefully.

Harness and Holt took off their jackets and wrapped them around the girls, seating them together on the boat's small front seat. Aaron managed to squeeze in next to the men.

"The President?" he asked, shivering. "I-is he okay?"

"A little shaken up, but fine," Harness said. "Commander Byrd of the *USS Hampton* called to apologize for his staff. I guess they took a pretty good hit from *something*, but there was no real damage. Were the three of you on board the Cobra submarine?"

"We were," Aaron said.

"How the hell did *that* happen?"

"We were all invited to the same party," Aaron said.

"Was Jason Souther aboard, as well?"

"He was."

"Did he get out?"

"No," Aaron said. "He didn't get out." He looked at the girls. "Other than the three of us, there were no survivors. Cobra and her crew are dead on the bottom."

The girls were exhausted and numb with cold, and Harness kept them as warm and dry as possible as they motored back up the bay toward the MMSD.

Chapter 67

Back on land, Officer Holt broke into the MMSD gift shop and scrounged some dry clothes for the survivors. Detective Harness used the museum's small kitchen to prepare them a late dinner of grilled cheese sandwiches and hot tomato soup.

The men left the three alone for while, checking in on them from time to time, figuring they needed time to gather themselves and come to grips with what had happened to them. As soon as Harness was sure the survivors were well on their way to recovery, he and Holt returned to the room and sat down with them.

"I'm Detective James Harness, by the way," he said. "This is my partner in crime, Officer Larry Holt." He gestured to Holt.

Holt nodded respectfully.

Harness looked at Ashley. "Aaron and I met previously," he said. "You must be his sister."

Ashley blushed. She assumed Harness was kidding, but he did have a certain charm about him, and she appreciated the flattery — at her stage in life she took whatever she could get.

She looked at Aaron and smiled. "How did you guess, Detective?" she said, offering Harness her hand.

"Please, call me James," Harness said, kissing the back of her hand.

His unshaven face was a little scratchy, but not unpleasant. "I'm Ashley," she said.

Aaron remembered his manners. "This is Katya," he said, putting his arm around her.

"Hello, Katya," Harness said, thinking, *If Aaron's with you, he's a lucky guy.*

The group engaged in small talk for a few minutes and presently the conversation turned to the assassination plot.

"I bet you didn't know the assassins had planned on using a nuke," Aaron said.

"A *nuke?*" Harness said. "What the hell are you talking about?"

"The conspirators *thought* they were firing a nuclear warhead at the President," Aaron explained. "But I got really lucky and was able to make the switch to the dummy torpedo."

Harness could only stare at Aaron for a moment, thinking, *How on earth could you do that?* "Well done, Aaron," he said at last. "Extremely well done. I'll see that you are commended."

Aaron hesitated. He knew he'd been incredibly lucky to have gotten away with killing Johnny Souther two years ago, and he thought it best to continue keeping a low profile.

"If it's okay with you, Detective, I'd rather remain anonymous on this one. And I'm sure the ladies feel the same way."

The girls looked at each other and nodded.

"Whatever you wish," Harness said. "But if it's all right with you, I need to ask a few more questions."

Aaron was exhausted, but he figured he owed Harness. "I'm listening …"

"Did you know that after plowing through your Aston Martin, that son-of-a-bitch Jason Souther drove straight to Sally's Diner and gunned down his brother Johnny?"

Aaron swallowed hard and looked at his mother. "Really?"

"Yeah, and why the crazy bastard couldn't just walk through the front door, I'll never know. He blasted Souther from *outside* the diner through the damn window — with *two* assault rifles, no less, like some kind of Rambo or something."

Aaron and Ashley listened, but didn't say a word, figuring what Harness didn't know wouldn't hurt him.

"Sadly, when I confronted him, he killed my damn partner," Harness said. "I've been looking for Jason Souther for over two years now ... two very long years."

"How will you ever know for sure you got him?" Aaron asked. He looked at the girls. "I mean, *we* know he's dead, but how will you?"

"I'll take your word for it, for starters," Harness said. "And we'll probably attempt to I.D. him when we float the sub — you know, to please the lawyers."

CAYMAN ISLANDS
THREE MONTHS LATER ...

Chapter 68

Aaron Quinn leaned over in his woven banana-leaf lounge chair and tossed a tortilla chip in the direction of a brown-spotted Rock Iguana, an indigenous Cayman Brac lizard that had just scurried across a nearby slab of rock.

"You're going to make him fat," Katya said.

"A little salt won't hurt him," Aaron said, "and it looks to me like he could use the carbs."

Katya laughed, and Aaron refilled their glasses from an iced pitcher of Mojitos.

Aaron's mother came up the seashell-strewn path from the beach and approached their thatched-roof bamboo hut, taking a seat next to him.

"I've been meaning to give you something," she said. "I've been keeping it safe for a long time, yet never knowing why, or for whom. But now I know I was saving it for you."

She handed him a small, dog-eared photo. It was the snapshot of Ashley hugging Aaron's father, Danny, in the alpine meadow.

Aaron held the precious photo gently between his fingers. "I remember handing this to you in the car, right before —"

He stopped himself as suddenly he was back in the Aston Martin. Michael was driving, and Willy was in the back seat with his mother. Three of the most important people in his life had been snatched from him in a ball of fire. And then, through an almost unimaginable set of coincidences, one of them was returned to him.

He gave his mother a warm hug, and then clutched the photo to his chest. "Thank you," he said. "I thought I'd lost it forever."

Ashley stood and looked up and down the beach. "Speaking of lost," she said. "Have you seen James? He's late for dinner again."

"I think he's down at the Holt's," Katya said. "They've been pit barbecuing a pig since yesterday and I guess he wanted to make sure they were doing it right, and that they weren't planning on eating the whole thing themselves."

Aaron laughed at the image of Larry Holt and his wife sitting down to eat an entire barbecued pig.

"That's my James," Ashley said. "Always the teacher. I may have to walk over and check that out for myself. You two love-birds enjoy your evening."

"Thanks, Mom," Aaron said, then watched her walk down the path leading through a grove of palms to the Holt's beach hut.

He sat back and took a sip of his drink, watching the sun as it fell slowly toward the sea.

He had been delighted to hear that his mother had fallen in love with James Harness, and that they had been married, and that they had talked Larry Holt and his wife into coming with them to the Caymans to be near Aaron and Katya. Together on the island, they had become the close-knit family Aaron had yearned so deeply for.

Harness had been true to his word: His official police report made no mention of him, Ashley, or Katya; and as

Aaron had requested, James had sold the *Cayman Jewel* anonymously, at auction, with the proceeds going to a home for wayward boys.

"If you'd like I could help out down at the dive shop tomorrow," Katya said, bringing him back to earth.

"That'd be great," Aaron said. "There's a cruise ship coming in, and we're expecting a lot of business. I'll be spending a lot more time there myself, now that we own the place."

"You know, Aaron," Katya said. "You really don't have to work for a living anymore."

"I know," Aaron said. "But I work because I like helping people. Earl's Reef allows me to do that, and owning it is something I've dreamed about for a long time."

"Read the letter again," Katya insisted.

"I've already read it to you like a thousand times," Aaron said.

"Pleeease," Katya said, giving him her best pout.

Reluctantly, Aaron pulled the folded letter out of his shorts pocket.

"I just like hearing it," Katya said, sitting up.

Aaron unfolded the paper and read it aloud:

Dear Mr. Quinn:
This certified letter is to notify you that you have been named legal beneficiary of the Trust Fund of one Michael Lee St. John, in the amount of $40,000,000. Amount secured by his attorney and deposited in an account in the name of Aaron Daniel Quinn.

"I still can't believe it's *real*," Katya said. "You told me that Michael had written a sequel to *Saturday Night Crash,* but I never expected it to become a *blockbuster hit.* It's *incredible.*"

"Michael had just finished writing the sequel when I met him," Aaron explained. "And he must have had some sort of premonition, because he wrote me into his will within three days of meeting me — just before he died. It took years to get the film made and into theaters, and then the lawyers took time to get Michael's film royalties straightened out and into his trust fund, and eventually to me. It's a miracle it happened at all."

"And with Earl's Dive Shop coming up for sale, the timing couldn't have been better," Katya said.

"I know, and with you coming into my life ... Never in my lifetime will I ever begin to thank Michael for what he did for me."

"I didn't know writers could make that much *money,*" Katya said.

"Well, when you consider film rights, and the effects a blockbuster hit has on book sales, it starts to add up," Aaron said. "I expect to be receiving royalties and residual checks for a long, long time."

He refilled their glasses from the pitcher of Mojitos again, and together they watched the sun dip slowly into the Caribbean.

"Do you remember our first time together?" Katya asked, her skin glowing off the warm sunset.

"How could I forget?" Aaron replied, smiling. "We were on a picnic blanket on the beach in Glorietta Bay." He reached over and curled a few strands of her hair around his index finger. "If the tide hadn't decided to come in, we'd probably still be there."

Katya laughed, and then she looked at him, taking a seductive sip of her Mojito. "You know, Aaron," she said softly. "I still have that blanket. What do you say we drink up and try it on for size?"

~~~~~~~~

About the Author

John Avery lives with his wife, Julie, and their horses, dogs, and chickens, on a small ranch in the mountains outside San Diego – where he is currently hard at work on his next story.

John thanks you for reading BLACK COBRA, and he sincerely hopes you enjoyed it.
If you haven't already done so, you may want to check out the first book in the Aaron Quinn series:
THREE DAYS to DIE.

John loves to hear from his readers. If you'd like to contact him, you may drop him an email at:
john@johnaverybooks.com

You can also visit him online here:

johnaverybooks.com
facebook.com/BlackCobraBook
@johnaverybooks

BLACK COBRA is published by Apticon Books in ebook format, and (for those who prefer a more traditional reading experience), in beautiful, glossy trade paperback. If your friends don't have ebook readers, they can download the free Kindle Reader from Amazon and read this and countless other ebooks on their preferred device, such as the Mac, iPad, and iPhone, as well as most PCs and Android devices.

Bookstores and retail outlets interested in carrying BLACK COBRA may contact us directly by email at:
info@johnaverybooks.com

John Avery would like to thank the following for their kind and generous assistance in the creation of this book:

Maritime Museum of San Diego
Mr. Jeff Loman
Mr. RD Baker